Stanislas M. Yassukovich was born in Paris of a Russian émigré father and a French mother. The family went to America in 1940, and Stanislas was educated there at Deerfield Academy and Harvard College. He served in the United States Marine Corps and then moved to England in 1961, where he pursued a distinguished career in the City of London – becoming known as one of the founders of the international capital markets. On retirement, he moved to the Luberon region of Provence in Southern France, and he now lives in the Western Cape, South Africa. For services to the financial industry, Stanislas was made a Commander of the Order of the British Empire. He is a Fellow of the Royal Society of Arts and a Freeman of the City of London. His previous works, *Two Lives: A Social and Financial Memoir, Lives of the Luberon, James Grant*, a novel, and *Short Stories*, a collection, were published by Austin Macauley Publishers in 2016, 2020 and 2021. Stanislas is married to the former Diana Townsend of Lowdale Farm, Mazoe, Zimbabwe, and they have three children: Tatyana, Michael, and Nicholas.

To my sister-in-law, Mattie Holme.

Stanislas M. Yassukovich

A CAPE TOWN DECAMERON

AUSTIN MACAULEY PUBLISHERS™

LONDON ∗ CAMBRIDGE ∗ NEW YORK ∗ SHARJAH

A CIP catalogue record for this title is available from the British Library.

ISBN 9781398436329 (Paperback)
ISBN 9781398436336 (ePub e-book)

www.austinmacauley.com

First Published 2022
Austin Macauley Publishers Ltd®
1 Canada Square
Canary Wharf
London
E14 5AA

In the spirit of the original Decameron, I created a virtual crowd of house guests, all required to shelter from the Covid-19 pandemic. Rather than exchanging tales amongst themselves in the Tuscan countryside, they read my tales in the security of lock down at their multi-national residences. I am grateful for the time they took and the comments they made. I also owe a debt of gratitude to my son, Michael Yassukovich, who so carefully selected this number of tales from my ill-disciplined output. The evocative painting on the front cover is by Douglas Powell, who did research to discover a nineteenth-century depiction of Boccaccio's fictive Tuscan house party, and then rendered it as a Cape scene. I am very appreciative of his effort. As with past works, my publisher/editor Austin Macauley in London has coped well with the geographical distance between us and deserves special thanks.

Introduction

In the year of our Lord 1348, the bubonic plague struck Florence. Statistical comparisons with COVID 19, or the Chinese pox as it is jocularly known, are moot. Certainly, the plague was far deadlier than our recent pandemic. It is estimated that three quarters of the City's population died. Life in the fourteenth century was far simpler than ours and carried on by fewer people. The economic impact was minimal, compared to what we of the twenty-first century will no doubt witness. The recovery from disaster was probably much prompter. When we appreciate the great impact of the Renaissance on Western civilisation, we take little account of the cost in human lives of the bubonic plague and other diseases that ravaged the known world at that time. But we are reminded of this by one great literary masterpiece of the period: Boccaccio's *Decameron*.

Giovanni Boccaccio was born in 1315 in Certaldo, Italy and died in the same city in 1375, after periods of residence in Ravenna, Naples and Florence. He was the illegitimate son of a merchant and banker called Boccaccino di Chellino and was first apprenticed at his father's bank in Naples. But he disliked banking and asked his father for permission to study law. He felt even less affinity with that profession and finally embarked on a long literary career, writing poetry and prose in Latin and the Tuscan dialect. He befriended Petrarch and achieved considerable renown, pioneering a more realistic approach to dialogue and narrative in general. A popular work at the time was his compendium of biographies of some hundred celebrated women in history. But his book which has more than stood the test of time, is the *Decameron* which posits the escape from plague ravaged Florence by a group of ten gentlemen and three ladies of high birth and education, to a country estate nearby. There they entertained themselves not by playing bridge or canasta – or even croquet on the lawn, but by recounting tales. There are one hundred in all, but the few that are best known in modern times are those with an erotic theme. The stories cover a wide range of venues, characterisations, and themes, and give us a vivid glance into contemporary lives and *mores*. Of course, they are all authored by Boccaccio, but he offered the fantasy that each of the company had a gift of storytelling, which helped set the mood of one of the most celebrated house parties in literary history.

When the coronavirus pandemic set the world on it ears in March of 2020, we went into 'lockdown' in South Africa – a prophylactic reaction still controversial as to its mitigating efficiency. It occurred to me that, in the absence of being able to collect a group of friends on a country estate, I might be able to create a virtual equivalent – just as modern technology was allowing us to play virtual bridge on our computers. My dozen or so friends would gather in the address line of my emails, still enjoying the comforts of their own home. And so was born the idea of a Cape Town Decameron – *pace* Giovanni Boccaccio, and with not the slightest pretence of coming close to his literary excellence.

First Tale

No Fit - No Game

Jasper Jakes was a creature of habit, a condition he relished and protected in all circumstances. 'Habitual' would have been the correct adjective to apply to his every action, thought, emotion – indeed to every aspect of his life. He rose at the same time, showered and shaved at precisely the same interval before breakfasting at a precise hour with not even a second's deviation. He wore a double-breasted pin stripe suit, alternating between dark blue and grey; a cream silk shirt and the tie of one of his two clubs. And each alternative was assigned to a day. Monday was grey, Tuesday blue, etc., etc. He lunched every day at one club wearing the tie of the other club and vice versa. He enjoyed this little contrariness, because it was habitual, and nothing would have persuaded him to change it. He would be at the club bar at precisely one fifteen, take a dry martini straight up with a twist of lemon at one club and lunch at one thirty on grilled sole, leaf spinach and Stilton cheese, and two glasses of white wine. At his other club the next day – at the same time, of course – he would take a pink gin, lunch on lamp cutlets and broccoli, cheddar cheese and two glasses of claret. After lunch, he would read *The Times* at one club and *The Telegraph* at the other. He considered this dietary variation as useful to his health. He took a holiday each year in early September, having a gun on the same grouse moor, with the same loader and the same retriever to pick up. He wore the same tweed shooting suit each year – the elbows now patched with leather and in the evening a dinner jacked turned slightly green with age. At weekends in the season, he hunted the Saturday country of a modest West Country pack, staying at the same inn, in the same room, mounted on the same horse, changed for another by the same girl groom in the same livery yard, when the first went lame or aged. His habitual black coat was now almost also green with age, and he wore a threadbare silk top hat.

Jasper was hardly an interesting conversationalist. Whatever the subject, his view would not have changed since the last time you raised it with him. If he initiated a subject himself, which was rare, you were bound to recall that he had raised the very same issue the last time. His was not the witty exchange of views most club men of his class like to attempt with varying degrees of success. As for the ladies, these tended to divide into two categories. Jasper's looks and gentleman like comportment assured him dinner invitations – single men becoming a rarity, while widows and divorcees abound, causing hostesses to be less particular. One category of dinner companion welcomed his taciturnity, being otherwise annoyed by over-pressing men. The other deplored his lack of conversation and quickly turned to their neighbour on the other side. It was therefore a profound source of amazement in Jasper's circles when a lady named Veronica Veryfair (an unusual but descriptive appellation) showed signs of being attracted to Jasper, going so far as asking hostesses to send her down to dinner with him. Miss Veryfair was an exact opposite to Jasper. She was flighty, erratic, eccentric, disorganised, unpredictable, but witty, very pretty and extremely popular. Jake had no particular fortune; his looks were distinguished rather than handsome in a film star manner, and his charm, if he had any, was very well disguised.

Nevertheless, their association became increasingly intimate, and they were more than frequently in each other's company. Hitherto, Jasper's evenings have assumed his usual habitual pattern. His housekeeper left him soup (always vegetable) in the fridge, which he heated up and consumed with buttered toast in front of the fire – wearing an old velvet smoking jacket over his lounge suit trousers, with a silk scarf, having removed his collar and tie. Now he was seen in night clubs, on the dance floor, at a discreetly positioned table in silent conversation with Miss Veryfair, and a bottle of Mumm champagne. The curious ones who approached their table swore they could not overhear a word being exchanged. At dinner parties, they were now invited as a couple. Then Veronica took to joining him out hunting on a hireling, and staying at the same hostelry, but no one knew whether in the same room, although friends joined them for dinner. Here their contrasting personalities became glaringly apparent. Jasper hunted quietly. He took the same relative position when the field was halted as hounds were being cast in a covert. After a find, he always seemed to get a way in the same order – not too far in front, but not trailing at the rear. He jumped the same fences and went around others, always the same. He was a courteous gate opener and shutter. But he engaged in no covert – side chat.

Veronica was a different practitioner of the noble art of venery. Restless, voluble, aggressive – rushing about at a canter when the field was still, chatting at the top of her voice and generally being a nuisance. When hounds ran, she was a galloping fury, taking her fences on the heels of those in front, and threatening to run over the hounds to the point where our venerable master, who hunted the hounds himself, had to shout – in the hearing of all:

"Miss Veryfair! I beg to remind you that the order of hunting is as follows: fox, hounds, huntsman, field master, field. Will you kindly bear this in mind and keep your appropriate distance?"

But her incessant chatter could not be silenced even when the master shouted at her from inside a covert that he was drawing. "Please, be quiet, Miss Veryfair!" Jasper gritted his teeth.

Still, they were married – in late August – generating little surprise from those who knew them in town, but some raised eyebrows from those who had witnessed their incompatibility in the hunting field. The wedding was at St Augustine's in Queens Gate, attended by Veronica's large family, and Jasper's mates from the clubs. Jasper maintained a decorum more suitable to a memorial service, and Veronica brayed, as if at a girls' school matriculation. The reception was at the Connaught Hotel. The honeymoon was spent on Jasper's grouse moor, where Veronica wrestled in competition with the dogs picking up shot grouse – much to the loaders' displeasure and the dogs' astonishment.

Back in town, things seemed to be set fair, if not very fair – to pun outrageously. Veronica decided to give up hunting to concentrate on the total re-decoration of Jasper's charming and commodious flat. Regardless of the depredation of Jasper's favourite nooks and crannies, this aggravation might have passed, submerged by connubial bliss. Then Veronica decided they should take up a bridge – an occupation which would place less strain on Jasper's meagre resources in the way of conversation. He was already a moderate bridge player who kept religiously to the conventions and rules, bidding cautiously, and playing his hand carefully – always conscious of the spirit of partnership which is supposed to be an important tactical aid. Veronica attacked the game with gusto, throwing caution to the wind in her bidding, double jumping with minimal points, over - calling recklessly, responding mindlessly, failing to return her partner's bid and led suit, and frequently revoking with giggles of apology.

Whilst the charm of her relentless gaiety forestalled the discomfort of others at the table, Jasper looked grim and fell even more silent.

At home, Veronica never breakfasted before ten, muddled her engagements with the ladies who lunch, kept the house in disarray, sent the wrong suit to the cleaners, smoked in bed, drew complaints from the neighbours playing the gramophone at top volume, and insisted on being taken out to dinner in smoky, basement Italian eateries in the King's Road. Friends would turn up that she had forgotten she had invited, and engagements would be missed that she had forgotten to mention. No one day had the same pattern and no evening the same programme. Jasper's equanimity in the face of a total destruction of his highly habitual life reached the limit of tolerance. One morning, he drew a deep breath and said in the quietest of tones:

"Veronica, my darling, I love you as I could love no other woman. However, I am as the harbour in a storm, and you are the raging sea; I am a stalk of maize and you are a rambling rose; I am a lumbering hippopotamus and you are a fleet gazelle; I am an oasis of calm, and you are the gusty winds of the desert. We are not suited and must part."

Veronica stubbed out her cigarette, paused and said: "Jasper, my sweet, I love you as I could love no other man. But…you are a dry stick, and I am the lily of the fields; you are a tower of strength, and I am a Disney castle; you are an oxcart, and I am a Lamborghini; you are a grey morning, and I am a rosy hewed sunset. We are not suited and must part."

With this ease of agreement, the divorce was quick and painless. Jasper returned to his habitual bachelor life, and Veronica moved to Switzerland – for reasons that were less than apparent.

Some two years passed before a notable event. Jasper suffered a bad fall while hunting and spent weeks at his country inn recovering from serious injuries. The doctors opined that the craniocerebral trauma involved – or concussion to the layman – was sufficiently extreme that, although not life threatening, a personality change might be a consequence. And so it was. On his first morning back in town, Jasper breakfasted at 9:30, omitted shaving, dressed in a Prince of Wales check suit he had had made for racing, and a bow tie. At his club, he drank a pint of champagne in a silver mug, had broiled kidneys, broccoli, and a fruit tart for lunch, washed down with a large glass of Guinness stout. In the afternoon, he went to an exhibition of the erotic paintings of Egon Schiele. He then invited a former bridge partner, an exotic American lady called Beatrice

Brimmerhaven, to the theatre followed by a nightclub supper, and dancing until two in the morning. On the next day, he donned a blue tweed suit and brown suede shoes, drank an old-fashion cocktail at his club, but lunched on oysters and cold lobster at Wilton's, spent the afternoon at the British Library, and asked a casual friend, Princess von Letternicht zu Mittgenstein, the former Miss Schlitz of Milwaukee, to dinner at the Ritz.

Now, instead of bridge, he joined a poker game organised by a well-known boxing promoter and his theatrical friends. To the disgust of his friend, the West Country MFH, Jasper went out with a drag pack of bloodhounds which followed a laid human trail over a dangerous cross-country course. Instead of his holiday on the Scottish moors, he went off to India to shoot duck in the Punjab. Jasper had indeed undergone a major transformation and was now known as an eccentric man about town with a designer stubble, shaggy hair, and louche acquaintances.

One evening, a friend mentioned that Veronica Veryfair was back in London. It occurred to Jasper that it might be rather fun to see his ex-wife again. He discovered, on enquiring here and there, that she was staying at lodgings in St John's Wood. Telephoning her, he found her voice not immediately recognisable, but asked her to dinner that evening. She thanked him but declined - explaining that she never dined in the evening but supped on tea and toast and was in bed by nine o'clock. But she agreed to lunch, and they arranged to meet at an Italian restaurant in Beauchamp Place, much frequented by celebrities, which Jasper thought would amuse Veronica. He had some difficulty when his ex-wife was shown to his table – being confronted by a lady with her hair parted in the middle and drawn back into a bun, wearing a grey tailored suit with a Peter Pan collared blouse, ballet style pumps, no jewellery except a silver cross on a chain around the neck and no perceptible makeup. This was Veronica Veryfair – equally transformed. She ordered smoked salmon with scrambled eggs and ice water to drink. She then told her story. In Switzerland, she had met a retired film actor who had persuaded her to join the Moral Rearmament movement at their headquarters in Vevey. She was now an enthusiastic convert to its disciplines and spent her days helping at a Salvation Army centre in the East End.

The two fell silent in the noisy restaurant for several moments. Finally, Veronica looked intently at Jasper, in his blue blazer and khaki trousers, with his designer stubble and uncut hair and said, with light gravity:

"Jasper, my dear, I will always love you and I intend to love no other man. But it is clear to me that, once again – as when we played bridge, we have no fit between us and therefore no chance of a game." Jasper leant over the table, kissed Veronica on the cheek, and signalled the waiter to bring the bill.

FINIS

Second Tale

Blood and Money

Old Lady d'Abernon lived frugally but happily in a cottage in the Cotswold village of Ampney St Peter, a locale she liked to refer to as being in the 'Earl's country'. Of course, she meant the Vale of the White Horse hunt, whose hounds had at one time been amongst the chattels of Earl Bathurst of the Cirencester estate which had been gifted by Queen Anne. This entirely conscious slip of the tongue by old Lady d'Abernon often led to a reference to that monarch as 'good' Queen Anne, for, as an unreformed Jacobite, she deemed her – as a Stuart, to be the last totally legitimate queen. To say that Lady d'Abernon was old-fashioned was a truism that needed considerable qualification. Genealogically, she was a purist. Proud of her own Saxon origins, she had been born a Luxford; but she was equally proud of having married into an old Norman family – the d'Abernon (although in her heart of hearts, she considered William the Conqueror to be a *parvenu*). For her, old blood was everything, and she liked to remark: "As my good friend Captain Hignett (Master of the VWH) declares, 'as breeding is everything in hounds and racehorses, it would be distinctly odd if nature had exempted humans from this condition'." But Lady d'Abernon was very conscious of current *mores* and attitudes and would not have dreamt of expressing such a view, except amongst her closest friends. She was sympathetic with all popular sexual tolerations, considered herself totally colour blind, whilst privately admitting that she would prefer to dine with a hereditary African chief than with a Pullman porter.

She was a staunch defender of the voice of the people as expressed in the universal franchise. She claimed partisanship with the suffragette movement and women's rights in general, but perhaps not on the usual grounds. In her opinion, the evils of egalitarianism had always been largely propagated by men.

Her current domicile was the result of those traditional destroyers of wealth: inheritance taxes, poor financial planning and war. The rise in the cost of staff had rendered the upkeep of the family pile (with ten inside and eight outside) prohibitive. Nuncombe Priory, granted to the d'Abernon by the Conqueror, had seen many guises and owners. First a Norman castle, burnt and rebuilt several times, then lost to the family in the War of Roses, then acquired by a religious order, regained by the family under Henry VIII, lost again under Cromwell, and regained under Charles II. After countless transformations, its last was in the reign of Lady d'Abernon's 'good' Queen Anne. The First World War had claimed Sir Roger d'Abernon, and the next war, his heir Sir Edgar – our heroine's late husband. The place, which Lady d'Abernon had known briefly as a young married lady, had been occupied by a military garrison in the last war and sold soon after. The present heir, the umpteenth baronet Sir William, had disgraced the family by marrying a shop girl from Cirencester, but was now more that something in the City. His mother refused to move to London, and was happy in her cottage with a cook, maid and handyman who all came in from the village.

When hounds met near her village, Lady d'Abernon was in the habit of entertaining the master at tea, after he had seen his hounds boxed up. On this occasion Captain Hignett sat before the fire, eating crumpets, and drinking a whiskey and soda, in preference to the traditional beverage.

"So, William has bought the old Willsdon place? We all hoped he would spend his millions re-acquiring Nuncombe," began the captain.

"So did we all, Master!" Having ridden to hounds in her youth, Lady d'Abernon insisted on addressing her guest as such, rather than with his military title. "But that nasty Arab sheikh absolutely refuses to sell for any price."

"Actually, he's a prince, from the Saudi royal family," remarked the master.

"Upstarts! Not the Hashemite royal family, the only true Arab kings. Have you had dealings with him?"

"Not directly, but through his agent, Tommy Standish. We were at school together and in the same regiment. Of course, he hunts with us. He has tried his very best to get HH to allow hounds in, but no luck so far."

"And when I think of the foxes that we kept at Nuncombe! Why, even during the war, old Brockbank, the keeper, stopped the earths when hounds came in."

"Would you believe it, Lady d'Abernon, Tommy showed me a letter he had from his boss suggesting we keep the foxes down with falcons! He even offered to send a pair...and a trained falconer at his expense. It seems all canines, including hounds, of course, are seen as unclean in the Moslem religion. The prince claims he's keen on hunting, but only with falcons."

"Ridiculous!" said Lady d'Abernon. "The birds are full of lice, whereas your hounds are pristine."

"There's no accounting for religion, Lady A." The master paused, thoughtfully. "I hope William will come out with us again, now he has a place in the country."

"A good deal depends on that chit of a wife. I would imagine her social ambitions will help."

Lady D'Abernon, despite her presumed liberal views, had not reconciled herself to her daughter-in-law. To be fair, it was not her class – or lack of – that hardened the old dowager's heart. It was the fact that the current Lady d'Abernon, Shirley as she was named, was spending money faster than her husband could make it, was socially ambitious to a fault and had made not the slightest effort to show any affectionate regard for her mother-in-law. William had been persuaded to buy a property in Jamaica, a chalet in Gstaad, a grouse moor in Yorkshire, a safari farm in Kenya, a house in Casablanca, and now a 3,000-acre estate in the Cotswolds – all this to supplement the domiciliary comforts of a large town house in Chester Square.

"Well, I don't regard William as anything other than our very own – not your typical city hunting type." remarked Captain Hignett, "We have an increasing number of city types, many looking for a joint mastership to put MFH after their names before they can collect an MBE, or whatever. The money is most welcome, but they are useless with the farmers. They will turn up in Gucci loafers, sit in their spotless Range Rovers to put on gum boots to walk the few yards to the house, and having taken them off again, have not a clue as to what to say to the farmer." The master paused, looking into the fire, and drinking his whiskey. "Of course, I know the committee would be delighted to see William as joint master."

"Well, my son seems to have made a great deal of money. I'm not sure how – something to do with hedges, but not the kind we leap." Lady d'Abernon closed her eyes – no doubt to enjoy the hunting memories that were racing through her mind.

"It's the hedge funds, Lady A. Rather like the bookies on the rails laying off bets. Hedge fund managers hedge the risk of their investment positions in various complicated ways."

"Oh dear! My husband used to say that money made in a complicated way is often lost in a simple way."

On this note, the master took his leave, and Lady d'Abernon was left to consider the fact that her son's latest acquisition would bring them closer, and she must teach herself to be gracious to Shirley.

It was not long before the umpteenth baronet Sir William d'Abernon called on his mother.

"Mama!" he began, standing with his back to the fire. "You cannot possibly continue to live in this shack – and alone at night! Shirley quite agrees with me. I know you insist on staying in these parts. If that bloody Arab had been willing to sell me Nuncombe, there was the dower house, of course. But there's the whole East Wing at Willsdon for you – even with its own kitchen and pantry. That's the proper place for you."

"William, the proper place for me is where I want to be and that is where I am," said the dowager Lady d'Abernon, in an imperious tone.

"But Shirley thinks it's embarrassing – what will people say? They'll think we are poor, or to mean to accommodate my mother properly."

"My dear boy. I suggest you tell your wife that d'Abernons are not concerned with what people say or even think. As your father rightly used to say, 'never complain and never explain'."

"Papa lived in another world…"

"A better one," interjected Lady d'Abernon.

"Maybe so, but I have my standing in the City to consider. They don't care about Norman blood. Half of them are Yanks now, anyway. And Shirley…"

"I think you'll find, William, that as long as Shirley has your money to spend, she will have little to concern herself with."

"I wish you wouldn't be so hard on Shirley, Mama, she can't help her background and she's loving and loyal. She's starting to make lots of friends in London."

"Well and good, dear boy, I hope she understands how you make your money. I certainly don't."

"Mama, if you are willing to listen, I'll try and explain. It's rather technical. I manage a hedge fund. We buy shares for a rise, of course, but we protect ourselves by selling others short…"

"Short? What on earth is that?"

"We sell shares we don't have to buy them back at a lower price."

"Surely, that's dishonest," said his shocked mother.

"Not at all, short selling maintains market liquidity. Institutions earn money by lending us the shares to deliver to the buyers."

"Is that all?"

"No, we increase the performance by borrowing so that we can hold larger positions and provide a better return to our investors. That's called gearing."

"And you are well paid for doing this?"

"Very well paid, Mama. We take a 5% management fee, plus 20% of the gains we provide to our investors."

"And if there are losses, you pay the money back?"

"Well…no, actually. That's not how it works. You see, we put up the capital in the first place."

"But surely, so did the investors."

At this point Sir William, chairman and CEO of Bull/Bear Capital Ltd of Abchurch Lane EC 2, was becoming wary of his mother's unexpected understanding of financial matters and decided to veer from the subject.

"Please, don't worry, Mama. It's all above board and there are now many enterprises of the same nature. But now, Mama, I want you to give serious thought to moving to Willsdon. Shirley will be so happy, and she'll often stay in the country during the week."

"I doubt that my dear boy, but please tell her, I will help her any way I can to settle into Willsdon. She's not so familiar with large country houses."

William paid his *adieus* on what he considered a somewhat sour note. Of course, his mother was hopelessly old-fashioned and had never accepted Shirley. He wondered if it might not be awkward if they were thrown together at Willsdon.

Lady d'Abernon kept her cottage. Shirley soon called herself and tried, in a non-convincing way, to endorse her husband's entreaties.

"We would be so happy, Mother, with you as part of the family, and you know, you can stay with us in town rather than at that stuffy Sloane Club."

"My dear, it's the stuffiness I rather enjoy, and you know, I meet more old friends there. But take my advice, dear Shirley, you have not been married that long – three years, is it? A mother-in-law – even in the East Wing – is a bore. Young couples are better off without. I am as snug as a bug here. I'll see you as often, or not as you wish at Willsdon. William's chauffeur can always fetch me, and you are welcome here at tea whenever you like."

Shirley silently took offence to 'William's chauffeur'. She used Baines more than her husband and, indeed, considered most things hers rather than his.

William did take up hunting again and, at Shirley's insistence, accepted a joint mastership. The dowager Lady d'Abernon graced rather raucous dinner parties at Willsdon as often as she felt able. She could not help noticing that her fellow guests seemed to be mostly City and West End types rather than the country neighbours William had grown up with. She wondered how this could accord with his position as a joint master of the hunt. She decided to ask her friend Captain Hignett, still a regular visitor to her cottage.

"It's all a bit awkward," said the good captain. "If you ask me, its Shirley who's got it wrong. I think she is under the impression that people here will shun her because she is a shopkeeper's daughter from Cirencester. Good grief! There are gents marrying their girl grooms or their secretaries, and no one thinks twice about it anymore. I fear young Lady d'Abernon is a reverse snob!"

Regardless of the possible accuracy of her friend's opinion, our Lady A agonised over the question of a possible, remedial intervention. She had become almost estranged from her son, who now seemed curiously preoccupied during their infrequent encounters. He kept up his hunting, keeping a large string, walked puppies, and appeared at puppy shows and as many hunt events as possible. But one fine morning in late October, his world changed.

Cub hunting meets had now progressed to as late as 9:30, and hounds were allowed to give the cubs a short spin with increasing frequency. William was standing with a friend at covert side when his portable telephone rang.

"Don't let the master hear that!" said his chum, perhaps forgetting that William, as a joint master, might be allowed to carry one. William trotted off to a secluded corner of the covert, listened to his caller intently, and trotted back-ashen faced.

"Problem?" asked his friend.

"You'd better believe it. Tell Hignett I have to leave – emergency."

The dénouement needs little literary elaboration. The caller had been a colleague in his New York office, where it was three o'clock on that Saturday morning. On Friday, the New York Stock Exchange had crashed with a bang heard all over the world. The heavily geared positions of Bull/Bear Capital's Alternative Investment Fund were as wrong as they could possibly be. The collateral for its loans had evaporated, the derivative positions next to worthless, a sister, open ended fund swamped with redemptions – in short, very short, Bull/Bear Capital was ruined, as was Sir William d'Abernon, Bt.

It took William several months to clear out his property portfolio at distressed prices and repay his debts. An American bought Willsdon. To everyone's surprise, Shirley, the Cirencester shop girl, stuck with him with increased ardour, and adopted an almost extreme frugality.

She spent days with her mother-in-law, who now held her in admiration. William resigned his joint mastership, began whipping in as an amateur, took the horn on an occasion when the captain had a fall, eventually applied to become the paid huntsman on retirement of the last and was accepted, now sharing with the master. The couple took a modest house on the edge of a village. Shirley was appointed to the parish council and became active with the WI. William is now the only professional huntsman/baronet listed in Bailey's. The couple have two children and are amongst the most popular with all levels of local society. The Dowager Lady d'Abernon is still happy in her cottage.

FINIS

Third Tale

Resurrection

Everyone knows the national social security systems are basically bankrupt. There are far too many elderly folks on pensions and far too few youngsters contributing. The simple demographic solution would be more babies and shorter life spans, but neither is likely to evolve, except through the diktat of some euthanasia embracing dictatorship. The life span issue has seen some attempts, fiercely resisted, of course, to extend the retirement age. There are now legions of retirees keen to continue working, as with longevity has come improved health. But, alas, they do keep jobs from the young.

My very narrow vision of contemporary American life stems from visits to the Florida Gold Coast, named for the presence offshore of treasure laden Spanish hulks, frequently explored by divers with minimal pecuniary results. I'm sure the phenomenon is nationwide, but opportunities are provided for pensioners in Florida – so thick on the ground, allowing them the minimal amount of work allowed by the social security regulations. I was made aware of this when a wrinkled and clearly aged arm was extended from a motorway tollbooth to hand me my ticket. Glancing up, I saw it belonged to a white-haired old lady, clearly doing a shift to relieve the boredom of what might have been a lonely existence. The aged are largely alone and isolated in Florida. The three-generation family in one home, increasingly rare in Europe, is totally extinct in America.

A popular source of such temporary employment opportunities is the supermarkets, where in the parking lots, healthy geriatrics can be seen pushing trolleys laden with grocery bags and straining their backs to load them into cars belonging to young and fit ladies in halter tops and hot pants. Whether the employing supermarket requires physical tests of candidates, or simply has them sign injury claim waiver agreements – I know not. I imagine the attraction for this elderly, but still mildly libidinous, ersatz porters, is those young ladies in brief attire.

By common practice, this extra service is reserved for the gentler sex, or very old and handicapped men. Visiting Publix, a popular emporium in Hobe Sound, one fine day, I was a beneficiary because, recovering from a knee replacement operation, I was still using a cane. I could hardly help noticing and retaining an impression of my retired helper. He was quite tall, six feet two or three I would say, and only slightly stooped, as he might have been in youth. He had the usual, semi-permanent Florida tan on his legs and arms. He was wearing well-cut Bermuda shorts, old tennis shoes, and a short-sleeved shirt with initials embroidered on the breast pocket. His hair was grey and grizzled, but recently cut – but his face, and, indeed, his whole appearance, was strikingly marked by a black patch over one eye. Of course, few of us can avoid thinking of a wooden leg and a parrot on the shoulder when we see someone with an eye patch, even though it is quite common. Setting the patch aside, not easy to do in quick observation, his face was quite deeply wrinkled, but distinguished with a slightly aquiline nose, and deep blue eyes. Not being familiar with the process, I offered him a tip – a 1$ bill.

"Certainly not!" he said, in a voice which clearly indicated, even to the less initiated, a New England prep school education. "We are not allowed – quite rightly!"

As he moved off instantly, pushing the empty trolley, I could not enquire whether this prohibition, and his approval of it, indicated a personal preference or an endorsement of corporate policy. But as I watched him walking away, I was struck with that all-too-familiar feeling: 'he reminds me of someone, but I can't for the life of me think who!' And as usual with such an experience, it began to nag me. I was sure it was not the eyepatch. I knew no one who wore one except Baron Wrangle, a White Russian friend of my father's, who had succeeded as a male model - advertising Hathaway shirts. But I knew it couldn't be him. He had died many years ago. No, it was the general comportment, head, and voice that were familiar. Such strangers usually turn out to be just look-a-likes. But my curiosity about people has become difficult to control in later years, and I was determined to investigate.

At home, I could think of little else, but also realised that finding my volunteer porter would not be easy. They were all on shifts, I presumed, which one was his day? Would I have to wait a week? But then, of course, the eyepatch was an infallible mark of identity – I had seen no other pensioner porter at Publix so adorned. Naturally, it might have been due to a temporary condition – discarded shortly. Next day I was at the supermarket, bright and early, found a manager and asked if I could have the name of the old gentleman helping with groceries and wearing a black eyepatch.

"I'm afraid not, sir – not without his consent. But if you have a complaint, please come into the office and fill out the form and we will deal with it." The manager looked at me intently – trying to guess my motives.

"Certainly not – I have no complaint!"

"But the form lets you check boxes in a satisfactory service report, and we can show him that."

"No, that's all right – I'm bound to see him again." *Of course, it's all box ticking these days*, I thought.

"And then you can ask him his name," said the manager, with a customer service smile.

As I left, another trolley-pushing pensioner approached me.

"I couldn't help overhearing your talk with the manager," he said, in conspiratorial tones. "Are you looking for Jack Brooks? He's the guy with the eyepatch. He's here on Tuesdays and Fridays."

"Yes…of course, Jack Brooks…thank you so much, I recognised him the other day. He's an old friend," I lied.

"Shall I tell him if I see him?"

"No…that's OK, thanks!"

As I drove home, I was 'gobsmacked', as they say in the vernacular. Jack Brooks! I had not seen him since my Harvard days. He was a few years ahead of me, but a member of my final club, and I had seen him at several club occasions, when the graduate and undergraduate members mingle. I hardly knew him, and would only have exchanged a few words, perhaps – all those years ago. And yet I had recognised him! What on earth was he doing pushing grocery trolleys in Florida? I immediately interrogated my sister. Like Pliny the Younger who knew Rome but also much about Athens, my sister knows Jupiter Island, but also a good deal about Palm Beach.

After a moment of reflection, she exclaimed, "Palm Beach!" Of course, we went first to that weighty tome which is now the Social Register, originally a slim volume, and there was the listing: Brooks Mr and Mrs Jonathan W (Elizabeth Lanman) with a Boston address – rather than Palm Beach. Consulting my club book, I found his residence on joining was cited as Brookline (a Boston suburb). And I could confirm his age. Assuming he had graduated at 21, he was now 67. The next step was to consult a Palm Beach oracle, a friend of my sister's, who secretly edited the society column of the Palm Beach Post. We put her on loudspeaker.

"Jack Brooks!" She repeated. "Ah ha! Good question. Who knows? Disappeared like les *neiges d'antan* (the snows of yesteryear). Sold their house here a while ago. Elizabeth's in Boston – she has a house in France. There's a son, I think. I guess they are separated or divorced. I'm a great obit reader. I would have spotted it if Jack had died. No one's seen him for years. But there's a funny story about him, well…not so funny. Apparently, he was hit in the eye with the cork while opening a bottle of champagne and almost lost the eye…or did lose it…I don't remember." Of course, I had asked my sister not to disclose the reason for our enquiry.

This was all I needed to know. And I had no need to contrive an approach, because there is a fraternal greeting, particular to our Harvard club, which would make me instantly recognisable to Jack Brooks. I had only to be at Publix on a Tuesday or Friday. The next day was Friday, I went (armed with a shopping list) and there he was.

"Good Lord! … well, it was bound to happen." This was how he responded. His tone was entirely friendly but nevertheless tinged with some regret, or perhaps more accurately, some sense of termination – as if his isolation had been splendid but, like all good things, must come to an end.

"Do you live on the island?" he asked.

"No, I am staying with my sister."

"I live in Stuart. Let's meet there for lunch, if you are free. Tomorrow? There's a fish place near the marina."

And so, a date was fixed. As I drove home, having forgotten my shopping, I began to reflect that, until now, I had regarded the whole thing as comic. This was perhaps largely due to the story of the eye patch. After all, the popping of champagne corks is associated with hilarity and celebration. Formula One drivers spray champagne on each other. And co-incidences are also funny and are often the basis of humorous anecdotes. But as the classical symbols of theatre suggest, humour is closely associated with tragedy. The term tragicomic is highly suggestive. I felt I might be on the edge of a comic cliff looking over a tragic ravine.

The next day we met in Stuart. There, at the waterside, I had to banish the image of Long John Silver, which came to mind looking at Jack Brooks' black eye patch. He was dressed in white ducks and a seersucker jacket over a polo shirt. We began with generalities. He exposed a theory I was familiar with, that the constant expansion of the St Lucie Inlet and Indian River lagoon, for increased marina capacity, had altered the offshore ocean currents and was responsible for the persistent beach erosion on Jupiter Island. He remarked that Palm Beach did not suffer as much, and after all, it was merely a sand bar, like Jupiter Island, but ten times the size.

But then he said, "I suppose I must tell you, my story. I can tell it to you on a… (he quoted a convention of our club which treats communications between members with the confidentiality of the confessional) basis. The other person entirely in the know is my lawyer, who deals with all those admin things which plague us no matter how or where we live."

I will not quote Jack Brooks verbatim. He delivered his tale in an erratic manner, with pauses and changes of pace. It was as though in one breath he spoke with relief, in the next with reticence and in the following with a sense of shame. He confirmed that the champagne cork incident had first been seen as a joke – a joke for the witnesses and others who heard the story, but less and less for the victim. He had suffered half a dozen surgical interventions and treatments, with long periods of convalescence, before it was determined that the eye could not be saved. And this turned out to be a portent of further tragedies. With a partner, he owned and ran a large export/import business in Boston, specialising in fine wines and speciality foods. As an example, he cited the export of Vermont maple syrup, and Maine lobsters and the import of Caspian Sea caviar and French *foie gras*. During the long period of his absence from the business, necessitated by the eye condition, his partner had not only mismanaged the business, but engaged in serious embezzlement. The business had failed, and Jack became embroiled in expensive and futile litigation. To supplement his financial woes, an investment adviser, his wife had warned him against, turned out to be the architect of a Ponzi scheme, which cost the clients the sum total of their fortunes. The only bright spot in this constellation of misfortunes, was that his wife Elizabeth had her own fortune, and had not been seduced by the siren calls of super returns promised by the fraudster.

In describing these horrors, Jack kept insisting that Elizabeth had displayed no accusatory emotions, no hint of 'I told you so', no coldness, no lack of spousal support. On the contrary, hers had been a litany of sympathetic expressions of affection, her attitude one of empathetic solidarity and consolation. But – and here Jack began to relate the story with a growing degree of self-accusation – he decided that Elizabeth's hugely positive reaction to his disasters was in its entirety, an undiluted expression of pity. He could accept and cope with the disappointments of his financial collapse, he could face the scorn or the disinterest of colleagues, the bemusement of friends, but he simply could not face what he deemed to be the pity of his wife. And the more he analysed her behaviour, the more convinced he became that she pitied him. The more she denied it, the stronger his conviction. It fed on itself and could not be lessened even by a conscious self-examination, in which logic persuaded him he was suffering from monomania. Just as the drug addict is perfectly aware of his addiction and its nefarious effects, he knew he was misjudging his wife, but could not shake off the shame of being pitied by her. And pity was poison to him.

There was a long pause here, as Jack Brooks sipped his iced tea thoughtfully and looked out to sea.

"The stupid thing is," he recommenced, "amongst a lot of stupid things, is that I knew I should seek professional counselling, you know, a 'shrink'. But I couldn't stand the idea…pride, I guess. I kept thinking of that New Yorker cartoon, you may remember. This guy is lying on the couch and saying, 'My problem is, Doctor, that I can't get rid of the feeling that I'm boring people.' And there's the shrink sitting behind him, fast asleep. Our generation wasn't brought up to go to shrinks. Finally, I decided I should just lose myself for a while and I left a note for Elizabeth saying I loved her dearly, but I was going to do just that."

"I guess if you said, 'for a while'," I interposed, "she might have assumed you were coming back?"

Jack looked at me and smiled.

"I'm afraid you have got to the heart of the matter. You are right. Of course, she did – and I fully intended to – but an even stranger thing has happened."

Jack looked around, as if distrusting our safe isolation and confidential talk.

"Being alone is very difficult at first," he began again, "but after a while it becomes addictive. It's not just a question of a new habit you get used to – it's an addiction. You begin to resent any interruption. I have a nice black girl who comes in to clean – that's OK. But if someone rings the doorbell, I am annoyed. I have my daily routine and the idea of changing it is abhorrent to me. I lunch with one of my fellow pensioners from time to time, as I am doing with you. But

I don't invite them home (you would be an exception, of course). And I'm in charge of any routine change. I have thought endlessly about going back but I don't think I could face it. The more time goes by, the more difficult it becomes. Did you ever read that story about this guy on an offshore sandbar? He knows he can swim back to shore, but something stops him."

"How have you managed to avoid discovery? Didn't Elizabeth try to find you?" From Jack's narrative, it seemed his self-isolation had lasted some five years.

"Not at first. For quite a while, she respected my decision. But then the trail went cold. Of course, my lawyer kept mum. And now, with all this privacy regulation, it's very difficult to find people, even for a spouse or near relative. Our son is married to a Chinese girl and he's with Citibank in Shanghai. My lawyer tells me he's tried – no luck."

"But how come, no one has spotted you, as I did?"

Jack laughed and used a club expression which indicates the exceptional superiority of something. "Well, you know, we sold our place in Palm Beach some 15 years ago. I have sometimes spotted some Jupiter Island residents we were acquainted with in those days, but they wouldn't recognise me in a million years. I'm amazed you did."

We parted, with my assurances of absolute secrecy, and his promise to see me again if we met in the car park – but discreetly, he insisted. I could hardly avoid taking my sister into my confidence. She had been instrumental in my discovery, and we have shared secrets since earliest childhood. Her comment? "Isn't it strange that a man like that can totally misunderstand his wife?"

My sister likes to know where Floridians spend their summers. Back we go to the Social Register Summer Edition and Dilatory Domiciles. Here only Elizabeth Brooks was listed with an address in the Luberon region of Provence, France. I have a house in Luberon. I realise I have already tested my readers' tolerance for this most trite of all literary contrivances, by introducing the first coincidence in the Publix car park. But I hope they will give this humble teller of tales some degree of tolerance as I present them with a second coincidence – particularly if I give them an unqualified assurance that it will be the last.

In early May, I found myself back home in Provence. The Luberon region is known for the cosmopolitan nature of its permanent and holiday home residents, and it is also desperately social as a result. There are several Americans there, but I have never troubled to meet them all, and was unaware of Mrs Elizabeth

Brooks. But I have a Coptic Egyptian friend there whose life is a world wind of gregarious, social activity. I asked him.

"Elizabeth? But of course! Your compatriot – you do not know her? Perhaps you belong to different parties?" My friend Makram was convinced all Americans were hopelessly divided politically and had only intra-contact socially.

I explained I did not belong to a political party but there simply had not been any occasion to have met Mrs Brooks heretofore. Makram insisted he would give a dinner with such an encounter as its sole objective. Since he gave dinners for 20 almost once a week in the season, this was no difficulty. Soon I found myself with a group of a dozen or so, awaiting Elizabeth's arrival.

"She always comes last," said Makram, and after a moment or two I saw him rush to the entrance, which he had not done with the other guests. I could hear an affectionate greeting, and then Makram re-appeared, pushing a smiling lady in a wheelchair. The other guests, who clearly all knew her, went to greet her, and I was introduced by Makram saying, "I've put you next to each other at table, so don't exhaust your conversation now!"

When we went into dinner, Elizabeth was placed at one end for the convenience of the wheelchair, and I was on her right. I had put on a club tie, thinking this might be a good way of raising the subject of her husband which I needed to do with discretion, to avoid breaking my oath of confidentiality. It worked.

"I see you are a Harvard man," said Elizabeth, looking at the wild boar heads on my tie. "You must have known my husband, Jack, a fellow clubman, even though I suspect he was ahead of you. What class were you?"

I answered and agreed we were four years apart but, of course, I admitted having met Jack several times at club functions. Then I decided to be a bit devious – like any good spy.

"Will he be joining you here? I'd love to see him again."

"No, we've been apart for many years now. Tell me, where is your house?"

That was it. Elizabeth was clearly not anxious to continue any further reference to Jack. Our conversation now reverted to the usual social modalities. Elizabeth Brooks was a very good-looking lady for her age, which I reckoned was in the early sixties. She had entirely white hair, worn rather short in a fluffy style. Her complexion was typical of her genre – rather ruddy and attractively wrinkled, the product of the windy winters and sultry summers of the Northeast

31

coast of America. She spoke the unique American English of Boston, probably as close a rendering of the English spoken by the educated in its native country in the nineteenth century. Bostonians have a manner all their own, and they retain it no matter how long they sojourn in distant locales. Elizabeth Brooks was an iconic example. By the end of the evening, I had an invitation to call on her.

I took up that invitation more than once and she came to me once as well. She had a chauffeur who looked after her when she was out and about, and a Boston Irish maid who travelled with her. She soon explained her condition – a spinal injury as a result of a fall from rocks on the Maine shoreline.

"Do you know, there are good sides to every coin," she said to me at one point, "I was finding travel increasingly uncomfortable and a real bore! But now it's almost a joy! I get whisked through customs and immigration, put at the head of the queue everywhere, cosseted and settled in my seat and so on. I think it's so nice that a lot of people cheat and claim wheelchair assistance when they can walk perfectly well."

She also told me there was a faint hope of eventual recovery. There were great advances in nerve replacement and repair technology. She had special exercises and physical therapy, but she was not going to entertain false hopes and had adjusted to her new life.

Elizabeth made no further reference to Jack or the circumstances of their separation, and I was not going to take the risk of raising the subject, for fear that I might let something slip. There were family photographs in her house showing Jack and their son, and recent ones of the son, named William and called Billy, with his Chinese wife and two children. Elizabeth spoke of their expected visit to Boston from their Shanghai home. Even as we became good friends, I resisted the temptation to be untrue to my pledge, and Elizabeth did not test me by mentioning him. We did talk of Florida as I told her I had a sister on Jupiter Island – but she merely said she had never returned after selling their house in Palm Beach, as she enjoyed winters in Boston. This part of my quest was over.

Back in Florida in November, I immediately sought Jack Brooks again and soon came across him in the Publix car park.

"I met Elizabeth in France this summer!" I thought it best to be entirely up front.

"What?" Jack exclaimed. "You didn't…I mean, you didn't say…"

"Certainly not – not a word, even though I was tempted. But I must give you some bad news right away. Elizabeth is wheelchair-bound – a spinal injury after a fall from some rocks in Maine. There's a hope of some medical breakthrough for such conditions – but it's faint."

"Oh, my God! Poor girl! But how is she otherwise?" Jack leant back against my car and put a hand on his head.

"Pretty fair – I would say, and in very good spirits."

"Did she mention me?"

"Only to tell me you were apart. I was wearing a club-tie when I first met her – so of course, your name came up right away." I wondered if he would suspect my ruse, but he was still in some shock over the news.

"Listen…we can't talk here. Can you meet me tomorrow, same place?" and he turned away abruptly, pushing the trolley back to the store.

We met the next day in Stuart and Jack was looking wan and tired – I suspected a sleepless night. Five years of exile, the first news of his wife, and one night to digest it all, did not make for an easy repose. Those five years must have been a compacted weight on his ruminations. They must have run through his mind like a film sped up, with a collage of all the regrets and varying emotions which had marked those years. I found myself unable to say much of real import. I described Elizabeth's house, the Irish maid, her friends, and life in the Luberon. Jack listened and nodded from time to time. But he wasn't listening – he was thinking.

"I'm going back!" he almost shouted, looking first at the water and then at me. "I can't leave her without support. Billy is in Shanghai, probably for a spell. Elizabeth needs me – there can no longer be any question. You say there's a faint hope? I must be with her to wait and see. Good Lord! It will be like a return from the dead! She'll faint when she sees me! How will she react?" Jack's elation at his decision was now tempered by fears of how he would be received by his wife. I suggested he ask his lawyer to prepare the ground. Jack wondered why he had not heard news of his wife's condition from his lawyer. I suggested he ask him just that. I suspected Elizabeth might have wished it so. We talked on, and Jack asked for more details about his wife and her life – anything to cushion the shock of his momentous decision, and to soothe a mind strained by the pressure which had led to it.

We parted with promises of future reunions under happier circumstances, but I had to have a final word.

"I hope you will accept some advice from me. A bit of a nerve, I know but I have seen her the most recently."

"Of course," said Jack. "Fire away!"

"It's this: the very last thing Elizabeth will want from you is pity."

FINIS

Fourth Tale
Noblesse Oblige

Harry Gubbins sat back in his commodious office chair, lit his second cigar of the day with a silver Dunhill table lighter, and gazed complacently through his picture window at the perfectly framed dome of St Paul's Cathedral. Comfortable in this self-righteous repose, he gave himself a vigorous, imaginary pat on the back. Harry was a proud man – proud of the office he sat in; proud of the quality of his cigars; proud of his Dunhill lighter; proud of his office dining room and the chef who provided his luncheons; proud of the building which housed it all – the newest in the City. But in addition to these perquisites, symbols of his success, he was proud to be a member of the London Stock Exchange; proud to be respected in the City; proud to be talked of as a potential Council member – in fact he could not help thinking that the popular ditty *"for he's a jolly good fellow!"* might have been composed just for him.

But he also had another, and perhaps most important, source of pride, one not so rare in these days of self-made men, but no less precious. Harry Gubbins was proud of where he had started from – proud of his modest background. He was the son of the head gamekeeper on a Gloucestershire estate belonging to Lord W, MFH – and in fact was even a grandson. Naturally, Gubbins senior had brought him up to be the third generation at Willsdon, the estate in question. But the father had been disappointed in this and suspected that young Harry had been seduced by some City slicker gun on a shooting day, when acting as his loader. A contemporary TV series would have rendered this seduction as being of a sexual nature, but it was not. Whilst waiting for the high birds that the estate was famous for to cross over his peg, this City man had extolled the glamour and money-making possibilities of a City career to his young loader. The idea of making money whilst young enough to enjoy the flesh pots of London had struck a powerful chord, which resonated in the mind of the young man for some time and prompted him to make further research into this new Valhalla. He was soon sold.

When old Gubbins, with a tear in his weathered eye, informed his employer of his son's dramatic career decision, his lordship surprised him by indicating a degree of approval and a promise of support. Of course, the peer privately regretted the loss of a third generation of game keepers on the estate – the lad had been handy and useful on shooting days and had helped his father stop up on hunting days. And as Lady W, often remarked, the boy was very handsome in his estate tweeds. But the boy was also handy on the cricket pitch at his local prep school and Lord W was able to arrange his admission to the Merchant Tailors, a public school much supportive of social mobility (as indeed was his lordship). When the time came for young Harry to broach the walls of the City of London, an internship was arranged for him at a venerable merchant bank, one of the few without Continental origins. His lordship maintained a small family interest, and a nephew, the Hon. Peregrine, was junior partner there.

Young Harry Gubbins served his apprenticeship with distinction and the Hon. Peregrine was able to report to the W family that this son of a revered servant was doing honour to the estate with his industry. Harry did not enjoy the flesh pots of London so much, despite receiving encouragement from young colleagues, but rather devoted his spare time to the study of the City and its various compartments. He was moved from department to department at the bank, as are all interns, and he soon concluded that a career in merchant banking would only yield pecuniary results over a long period of time. Partnerships seemed to be reserved to family and friends – most of them already well off. Instead, young Gubbins discovered that the trading of stocks and shares was the business of the City that could yield immediate gains for the quick and clever. He might have reached the same conclusion about commodities, but his heart was now set on becoming a stockbroker.

By now Harry was sufficiently well-off to marry a childhood sweetheart from the estate who had no West End pretensions, and so they settled in a house in St John's Wood. And he began to realise his ambitions by convincing the Hon. Peregrine to transfer him to an apprenticeship with a firm of stockbrokers which did much of the merchant bank's stock exchange business. Here, Harry prospered and became conversant with the business of dealing in securities. But the hum drum routine of earning commissions for executing orders of clients impressed him little and did not appear to represent the key to early riches. He decided he must be in the business on his own.

Amongst his new colleagues, Harry had befriended the young scion of a financially embarrassed but noble family who was in the City in the hopes of restoring the family fortune and repairing the leaking roof of its stately home. The Hon. Crispin Smith-Stanley, heir to Lord B down in Dorsetshire, was easily persuaded to join Harry in setting up a new firm and, better still, was able to lay hands on funds from friends to provide the necessary capital. With the help of the Hon. Peregrine back at the bank, sponsorship was provided to give the new firm of Gubbins, Smith-Stanley & Co entry to the hallowed halls of London Stock Exchange.

Soon this new firm became established and functioning, with a box in Throgmorton Street and the minimal necessary trimmings. A pattern of business emerged – not the most typical model, but not unprecedented. Crispin would deal with the clients and execute their orders with the jobbers on the floor, and Harry would concentrate on own account dealing – mostly for the firm, but increasingly for his own personal account. The odd eyebrow was raised and Crispin, whose ear to gossip on the floor was well-attuned, expressed some concern to his friend and partner.

"I say, Harry," he began one day, "there's a bit of a buzz about us on the floor. They think our volume is rather high for a firm our size."

"What business is it of theirs, my lord?" Harry had taken to this premature form of address as a friendly joke – the two often joshed each other about their contrasting backgrounds.

"Well, keeper, own account dealing is supposed to be a small side-line to agency business and let's face it, the market is always ready to criticise newcomers. I wouldn't call the Exchange the most generous place in the world."

"I understand that Criss, but you're my passport to this brave new world, and you can keep your smart chums on the floor in line. We're doing OK, aren't we? The clients aren't complaining, are they?"

"No, certainly not but I'm just keeping you in touch with the gossip – firm's reputation and all that kind of thing."

Harry Gubbins might as well have added that he was doing more than OK personally, and he might also have expressed his innermost thought that his old Etonian partner was a bit too sensitive to reputation and not sufficiently concerned with profit. But he would not disturb a relationship of great value, and after all, Crispin had brought in all the private clients from his personal contacts.

Gubbins, Smith-Stanley & Co continued to grow and proper and, despite Crispin's rather reluctant approval, it moved to smart new offices and began to behave in a rather grand manner. It is here that we now find Harry with his second cigar of the day and his view of St Paul's Cathedral. It is also here that we see early signs of danger. As is so often the case, it began with an external relationship.

Harry had cultivated a friendship with a new tycoon whose modest background accorded in most, if not all ways, with Harry's. The big difference being that Harry's was rural and Billy Cockbird's was urban. Sir William, recently knighted for services to industry (and major contributions to a political party), was an East End lad who had early on fallen into bad company and served a term in a Borstal for a botched robbery. But reformed and ambitious, he had turned gamekeeper from poacher and started a security firm – first selling second-hand alarm systems at cut prices, but then growing through acquisitions to be one of the largest security companies in the land, with an international presence.

The growth of Consolidated Security Limited had certainly made Sir William Cockbird, its founding Chairman and Chief Executive, a City celebrity. But not one of spotless reputation, as some of his takeovers had been very contested and executed in less than an entirely regular fashion. He had been up before the Take Over Panel on more than one occasion. Crispin Smith-Stanley did not approve of his partner's friendship.

"OK, so he's hairy at the heel, my lord!" said Harry one day to his partner. "But then so am I, and there are plenty of tarnished silver spoons out there as well, you know."

"Come off it, keeper, you know what I mean. It's an association that does our reputation no good and we don't even profit from it."

But the result of the association and its apparently profitless nature soon became apparent.

One day Crispin stormed into Harry's office. "Listen, keeper, Joe Levy, the jobber, is complaining we're picking him up in Cons Sec shares. You've been dealing PA, haven't you? And Joe says you're buying before corporate actions and profits are announced. Everybody knows we're insiders."

"Calm down, my lord!" countered Harry. "We are not insiders. We are not brokers to the company, we have no mandate, no agreement, no engagement letter – that's purposely so we can deal in the shares."

"But that's a technicality. Everyone suspects Billy Cockbird is tipping you off. Joe is making a fuss."

"But it's perfectly legal. We are not insiders unless we are engaged, and people can check – we do not appear as brokers to the company."

"It may be strictly legal," protested an angry Crispin. "But it's not good form – it's just not cricket."

Here, Harry Gubbins smiled. But his smile soon turned to annoyance, and then to anger. Here was his posh partner teaching manners to the gamekeeper's son. Here was an old Etonian lecturing a minor public schoolboy. This son of a busted peer was taking to task Harry Gubbins, who was now worth millions from dealing for his own account.

"Well, my lord – not cricket?" Harry sneered. "I suppose those Aussies bowling bouncers at the batsman's head is cricket. Grow up, Crispin, the world is changing."

Soon after this angry exchange, the break between them came – much discussed in Exchange circles. Crispin Smith-Stanley decided the gulf between him, and his partner had grown beyond tolerance. Their ideas on how to run the business were in conflict. They were chalk and cheese. Harry's new wealth from his dealings had not calmed his acquisitive instincts but rather reinforced them. He became not wiser, but more reckless. He would listen to no one, not even his partner, and his journey towards the rocks accelerated. Crispin's farewell was emotional but, in fact, welcomed by both.

The stain slowly spreading over the firm of Gubbins, Smith-Stanley & Co had not reached Crispin personally, and he was able to re-join the old firm where he had first met Harry. In fact, his association with Gubbins, and its termination, had raised his City profile. His private clients went with him, and he did well with traditional business. He was soon able to repair that roof down in Dorsetshire. His father died; he was now truly 'my lord' and became master of the South Dorset. But things began to go very badly with what had now become simply Gubbins & Co. The suspicions of insider dealing led to no actual investigation, but the firm's reputation suffered fatal damage, and Harry's star fell from the sky. News reached Willsdon. His father, now retired, was broken in spirit, and Lord W spoke bitterly of betrayal of trust. Harry's wife remained true, and she persevered for the children's sake – St John's Wood was not a joyous place. Harry's dream was shattered and uncertainty over the future hung like a cloud over his little family. Gubbins & Co could hardly cover its overheads and worst of all, Harry's magic touch as a short-term share dealer evaporated. Losses simply bred more losses, and Harry had always been heavily borrowed. Gubbins & Co and its founding partner faced total ruin, and there seemed no escape but the proverbial loaded revolver on the table next to the carefully worded note.

Amid his suicidal depression one gloomy morning, the lift stopped on his floor and Harry heard a knock on his office door. The Sergeant from the Corps of Commissionaires, and his own secretary, had long since departed, so Harry went to open the door himself. There standing with his hand outstretched was Crispin, now Lord B, MFH.

"Criss! I mean, my lord, what on earth are you doing here?" Harry was genuinely taken aback but he hadn't forgotten his forms of address.

"Hello, keeper!" said a smiling Crispin. "Is that the way to greet an old friend? I should have walked right in. I know it's never locked in the day."

"Of course, I'm chuffed to see you, but why are you here? Not to gloat, I hope."

"Good grief, Harry. How you misjudge me. I'll tell you why I'm here – no beating about the bush. Twelve years ago, you were heading for the top, and I was nowhere. Now you're down and I'm up. I've got two proposals. First, we consolidate your debts, reschedule them, I take them on personally, and you repay me in instalments. Second, my firm – you remember it well – takes over the business and the Stock Exchange seat of Gubbins & Co and you join us as a half commission man, doing agency business only, and as a limited partner with no role in management. Take it or leave it."

It took Harry several moments to catch his breath and he could hardly speak.

"But Criss!" he finally croaked. "Why are you doing this? What have I done for you – except put your name in the City at risk by my foolishness?"

"What have you done for me?" said his Lordship. "I'll tell you what you've done for me. You gave me the chance to prove that I could hack it on my own as a principal. I could have stayed an employee for years. Even with your shady dealings…yes, I knew all about it, I learnt more about the business with you than I could have in 20 years working in a big firm. You were my mentor. Of course, I owe you now that you're down."

Harry began pacing around the room, shaking his head back and forth.

"Well?" said the new Lord B, somewhat impatiently.

Harry Gubbins stopped and looked out the window.

"But Cris…my lord, is this good form? Is it cricket?"

His former partner paused momentarily.

"Well, maybe not. But if you must call it something, I guess you could say '*noblesse oblige*'."

FINIS

Fifth Tale
The Clockmaker

Francis Obré was a clockmaker who could claim many generations behind him as engaged in the same trade. He lived in Dyer Street, Cirencester, in an old house above his shop, or studio as he liked to call it, for behind the shop was his workplace where he carried out his repairs. Of course, everyone else called it a shop, but Francis argued that he repaired more clocks than he sold. In the digital age, everyone bought clocks at the supermarket. The Obrés had been clockmakers since time immemorial. French Huguenots, they had fled to England after the revocation of the Edict of Nantes by Louis XIV. Like so many other artisans of that persuasion, they had first settled in Spitalfields, East London, and lived and worked in a house in Artillery Lane. By combining his own place of residence with his place of business, Francis felt he was following a family tradition.

It was Francis' grandfather who had moved to Cirencester. He had established the necessary equipment for carpentry, as well as for clock movement repairs, as he still made grandfather clocks from fine mahogany. His son, Josiah Obré, had been killed on the western front in the Great War, and the old man had carried on in Dyer Street into his 70s, apprenticing his young grandson, Francis, as soon as he left school. As the last of the line, Francis mourned the fact that he was no longer a maker, but essentially a restorer and repairer. Nevertheless, he was a proud member of the Worshipful Company of Clockmakers, one of the oldest of the City's livery companies.

Francis was thinking of all this and applying bees wax polish to a carriage clock mahogany case, when his shop doorbell tinkled, and the Honourable Jane Fotheringhay stepped in with a cheery greeting. She was the daughter of a newly created Labour peer, now married to a City banker who had inherited a small estate nearby. She and Francis had shared an amusing incident – perhaps potentially not so amusing for her husband. But it served as a link between them. Jane, the only daughter of the peer, had spent several years in New York as a fashion model and she certainly retained the looks that had so qualified her. A while ago, she had brought into the shop one of those small brass carriage clocks from Tiffany that are so popular as wedding presents. She had wanted it repaired and cleaned, and a new windup key to be found, as she had lost the original. Carrying out these instructions, Francis had noticed a little silver plaque fixed to the glass door at the back of the clock, which was now so blackened as to obfuscate any inscription it might have held. Francis had carefully cleaned it with a small rag dabbed from a tin of 'Silvo' polish and an inscription had duly appeared. It was: "Jane and Charles, June 1990."

"That's funny," Francis had said to himself. Mr Fotheringhay's Christian name is George. He had shrugged and waited for the Hon. Jane to pick up the item – which she had done the following week. Now, Francis remembered the incident with amusement, and could describe it in detail:

"Look what I have found, Mrs Fotheringhay," said Francis proudly, showing her the back of the clock.

"Oh, my God!" exclaimed the lady. "Oh, this is terrible!"

"I'm so sorry," said poor Francis, "but you did say to clean the clock."

"Can you inscribe over it?" asked a desperate sounding Mrs F.

"I'm afraid not. It's fixed to the glass, which will break."

"Can you replace the whole glass door?"

"I would have to order one from the factory that makes these clocks for Tiffany – it will take a while."

"Oh, dear!" said the Hon. Jane. "I had better explain. You see, the clock is intended as a wedding present for my husband's stepdaughter. He has seen it and thought we could use it even though it is second-hand. Neither of us noticed the inscription."

"But does it matter?"

"My dear, Mr Obré, I'm afraid it does. My husband will want to know who Charles is."

"I see."

"I had better explain – can I trust you to be discreet?"

"Of course, Mrs Fotheringhay." The wrinkles of dismay on his customer's beautiful brow were beginning to affect the clockmaker.

"I was married first in New York where I was working – rather briefly. I have never told my husband. It was all so foolish! I gave my wedding presents to my sister-in-law who had been kind and supportive during a difficult divorce. I can't think why this clock came back with me. How stupid!"

Francis was more affected by this expression of confidence than anything else and was overcome by a sudden urge to be generous.

"May I suggest something, Mrs Fotheringhay? I have several Tiffany clocks in stock, just like this one. Of course, I buy them on job lot discount. I will sell you one for say…150 pounds? They retail at 500. I will keep this one and give you a bill for its repair, cleaning, and the new key (which you do not have to pay.) In case your husband enquires. The new clock will look just like this one, cleaned. Of course, it won't have the plaque on the back, but you say your husband didn't notice it."

"Mr Obré, you have saved my marriage!" Mrs Fotheringhay leaned across the counter and kissed him on the cheek.

At the time, Francis had considered this an exaggeration – surely her husband could not be so unreasonable. But he had nevertheless accepted the kiss with pleasure. Now, some months later, here was Mrs Fotheringhay back in his shop, and Francis was dying to know how their little ruse with the brass clock had succeeded. But remembering his promise of discretion, he was reluctant to raise the matter. And the customer was carrying an intriguing cardboard box.

As she opened the box and began to remove the bubble paper around its contents, Mrs Fotheringhay explained. "We've been tidying the attic which is full of my father-in-law's things. Perhaps I should say rejects. Like this carriage clock which he seems to have discarded because it had stopped working. George says he was always rather wasteful – there are some valuable things up there. Anyway, we're having a good clean-out and selling some things at a local auction here. But I thought you might like this clock. We'd be happy to accept any reasonable price. I owe you a good turn – remember the Tiffany clock?"

What a lovely voice she has, Francis thought to himself. His next thought was that George Fotheringhay must be the opposite of his father, rather tight with his pennies. A rich City man giving second-hand wedding presents, and selling his father's things at an auction? Perhaps that is why he's rich. These ruminations passed with speed through Francis' mind as he began to carefully complete the unwrapping to begin an examination of the dusty clock in a stained mahogany case.

He opened the little front door, its glass clouded with accumulated dust. At the top of the face, in an oval circle is usually the maker's name. Francis Obré's heart almost stopped. *Jacot*! He looked again, rubbing a bit with his finger. Yes…there it was, in all its boldness – as if shouting at our poor clockmaker with pride. *Jacot*! Jacot – one of the most celebrated of French carriage clockmakers, an apprentice of the great Breguet, who had invented the carriage clock for Napoleon, who required a time piece for his carriage as he trundled about, plotting the conquest of Europe and the destruction of the old order. (Francis Obré was not very royalist but certainly not Bonapartist). Yes, Jacot! More than in a class with the great English makers like Dent and Frodsham, who had taken up the baton of carriage clockmaking from the French.

"Is it worth anything much? Cleaned up, of course?" asked Mrs Fotheringhay.

As Francis went through the motions of examination, turning the clock this way and that, looking at the back and then the front again, the worm of untruth began to wind its way towards his still palpitating heart. He had his hands on an antique clock worth thousands, a museum piece; he had in front of him a beautiful lady he was half in love with, whose silvery tongue was putting a simple question to him. His hands on the clock were beginning to shake; he held fast to disguise the emotions which were waging war in his breast. It struck him that he was confronted with a decision terrible in its simplicity, outrageous in its consequences for his conscience – the clock or the lady. No! Was it not money or self-esteem, illicit gain, or moral comfort?

Francis could almost hear the cackle of the devil, as he said – in a croaking voice he could hardly recognise, "Well…I could give you two hundred pounds, Mrs…er…"

"That is lovely…thank you so much!" interrupted Mrs Fotheringhay, before Francis could even pronounce her name. "My husband will be so pleased."

But her last words lifted Francis, and offered a droplet of balm to his conscience, because he suddenly realised that he was cheating her husband, rather than his beloved customer.

The odious transaction completed, Francis turned the *Opened* sign on his door to *Closed*, retired to his workshop, and poured himself a whiskey from a decanter he kept there. It might be eleven o'clock in the morning, but Francis needed a drink. What was he to do now? He could hardly put the clock, once fully restored, in the window for resale without either exposing his crime,

45

sacrificing the profit, or risking its discovery by some expert dealer. He was already suffering the angst of the burglar seeking to dispose of his 'swag'. Sale by auction in London was risky as the Fotheringhay's might receive catalogues from Christie's or Sotheby's. Dealers would ask for provenance. Of course, he would be under no obligation to disclose the risible price he had paid. But would the purchasing dealer's re-sale efforts not attract the very attention his own might?

So consumed with guilt, anxiety and indecision was Francis that he could not commence the work of restoring the Jacot carriage clock. This would entail carefully cleaning the dust impacted movement, the delicately engraved face, tightening the arms, fitting new keys to the doors and the winding mechanism, staining, and polishing the tulip wood case and the brass handle at the top, replacing the silk backing to the lattice worked sides – all work Francis was uniquely qualified to carry out. But a sense of shame began to gnaw at his professional pride. Should he resign from the Clockmakers Guild, citing the rarity of his London visits? Or should he donate the clock to its Museum and Library? Of course not! This would risk discovery.

Francis had no wife with whom he could share his emotional torment – to seek comfort, perhaps even advice – and to mitigate the strain he was under. He had never married, having failed to find a bride who shared his horological passion. After all, he had reasoned, would a saddle maker marry a girl who couldn't ride? A sail maker marry a girl who was seasick in a boat?

Finally, he decided he might drown his anguish in the cool and restorative water of expert craftsmanship. He began his work. His first port of call was the movement. As he examined it with his magnifying eye glass fixed, his brow furrowed. Something was odd here. This movement was far too modern. Could it have been changed in later years? This would destroy the antique value of the piece. In a cold sweat, he turned to the face, and began to rub the inscription of the maker's name vigorously, with a cleaning fluid-soaked rag. He staggered back in his chair in disbelief and looked carefully again with his eyeglass. There was a faint but readable circumflex accent under the 'c' in Jacot. Some ignoramus had rendered Jacot as Jaçot!

Francis was looking at a fake! A counterfeit! He had heard of such things before – antique dealers replacing the brass backing of clocks with another, suitably aged and a famous maker's name engraved. The antique trade is full of fakes but that he, Francis Obré, of the Worshipful Company and so forth, should be fooled!

Of course, he could not tell Mrs Fotheringhay for the shame of it, and without revealing he had tried to cheat her – or her husband. He reckoned that the 200 pounds he had asked for was close to a fair value. Of course, there were collectors who paid high prices for fakes, but this was for pictures, to impress friends, hardly clocks. He presumed the counterfeiter had been targeting dealers like himself. Of course, his guilt was not expiated, and was now joined by the blow to his professional pride.

Still, time, besides being a critical adjunct to his craft, heals all. Francis went back to business – chastened if still scarred. His business picked up, as did his mood, He sold a nice Hedge & Bannister carriage clock. They were prolific, early nineteenth-century makers, whose clocks sold nicely for several hundred pounds. Francis had handled a few. One day, in a relaxed evening by the fire, he picked up the semi-annual review of the Worshipful Company of Clockmakers, and read the following article:

Hedge re-discovered

Research by our own head of the Museum & Library, John Appleby has discovered that Josiah Hedge made at least five clocks of very high quality, on his own. The first of these was on commission from the first Duke of Marlborough, but he repeated the model four times, before joining Jonathan Bannister to form the famous partnership which began to mass produce carriage and other clocks. The Marlborough clock is signed Josiah Hedge, is still at Blenheim Palace and is priceless. But Hedge brought the other four into Bannister's workshops where the back plate was fitted and signed Hedge & Bannister. These can be distinguished as the winding key opening is on the right next to the III, rather than under the hands pivot over the IV (inverted, of course) as is standard in the later models. These early Hedge clocks are of significantly greater value than the stock Hedge & Bannister products – one sold recently at Christie's for 10,000 pounds to a dealer in Scotland who prefers to remain anonymous.

Francis knocked over his whiskey as he rushed to the filing cabinet in his workshop. He had a photograph of every item he had ever made, bought, or sold

– filed by category. He pulled out the sub section 'carriage clocks' and found 'Hedge & Bannister'. His hands shaking, he selected the most recent photo in that file. It was the clock he had sold last week for 750 pounds. It had the hole in which the winding key fits, on the right – next to the III.

Customers visiting the clockmaker's shop in Dyer Street can't help noticing that the owner's hair has suddenly turned white.

FINIS

Sixth Tale

The Aunt That Wasn't

Finding myself in London for a lengthy stay, I enjoyed the first night particularly because I had never spent a night there before. Born and mostly brought up in the Crown Colony of Hong Kong, I was now a permanent resident there. My previous London experiences had been day visits whilst at public school and the usual riotous excursions when I was an undergraduate at Cambridge. But I had never woken under a grey London sky and heard the cooing of pigeons blended with the rumble of the London traffic and its diesel perfume. The experience was novel and somewhat disturbing. No two cities sound alike, and the oriental cacophony of Hong Kong and Kowloon have nothing in common with the music of European Cities or the siren wails and honking rhythms of New York.

The projected length of my stay depressed me somewhat. I was in London for a visit to the office of my Hong Kong employers – a large trading house. But this was a business excuse, I admit, for my real purpose was to attend the memorial service of a close family friend who had been my guardian during most of my youth. My grandfather and my father had both gone to sea as lads, leaving widows rather early in life. Grandfather was killed in the battle of Jutland, and I have the vaguest memory of grandmama, living a lonely existence on a small property in Cumberland. My father was in the merchant marine before the Second War and then in the Royal Naval Reserve. His ship was torpedoed by the Japanese off Singapore with all hands lost. Before the war, he had been Master of a ship owned by a Hong Kong trading company, the same one where I was now a management employee. He had married a Scottish girl working at that company and I was born in Hong Kong.

When it was time to send me to a public school in England, a maiden aunt called Ethel, whom I hardly knew, took charge of me for my first holidays at her rather lugubrious house in Tenby – known as the dullest of all seaside resorts.

But my widowed mother arranged to appoint my father's best friend as my legal guardian. He had been in business in Hong Kong but was then retired on an estate in Hampshire, and he soon provided me with far more amusement than could be supplied by Aunt Ethel in Tenby – particularly when I went up to Cambridge. Having seen so little of my real father, who seemed to be permanently at sea when I was a child, I came to regard Uncle Max (who I had no relation with whatsoever) as my father. We were a family of the British Empire. My grandfather had two younger brothers; one had emigrated to British Columbia where he became the owner of a fleet of fishing smacks, and the other to South Africa, where he went into farming. I knew neither uncle, nor their descendants – my distant cousins.

At the memorial service of my erstwhile guardian, Maximilian Devereux, celebrated at St Mary's in Bourne Street, I saw few that I knew. Some old family retainers who remembered me, the family solicitor and a handful of Hong Kong acquaintances who had troubled to come, like me. I did glimpse Thomas Devereux, the son, but had no chance to talk to him in the crowded reception afterwards at the Sloane Club.

Now I was forced to admit that I knew hardly anyone truly native to London. The friends I had met at school, and at Cambridge, were widely dispersed and I had failed to keep in touch with them. I hoped I might run into one at my club. Uncle Max had put me up for this club when I had come down from Cambridge. Small but friendly, its members were mostly service and colonial types. Its patron was one of the minor Royals, and the chairman was always a retired admiral of general.

At the end of my first week in London, I did run into Billy Stanton in the bar. By a happy circumstance, he had been at Cheltenham with me, and also up at King's College, Cambridge.

"Hello, Jack, you old dog! What brings you to London? Are you still flogging opium to the Chinks?" was his irreverent greeting.

"You know jolly well, you old sinner – that stopped after the Boxer rebellion, but I'm here mostly for the memorial service of Maximilian Devereux, my guardian."

"Oh, yes…I remember the old boy, you took me down to his place in Hampshire. Are you lunching here?"

We lunched and exchanged accounts of our life to date, spiced with recollections of our youthful indiscretions. The harmless nature of these underplayed by the exaggerations of memory. We like to think we were naughtier than we actually were. Billy asked me to dine and meet his wife at their Chelsea house, which Billy described as a 'cottage small by a city wall'. The couple were childless, very London bound and keen on theatre.

"Don't you miss England way over there in Hong Kong?" asked Suzie Stanton, as she offered me a cocktail.

"Not really – it's strange – I just don't know it well enough to miss it. I only lived here at school and the university. That gives one a rather stilted view."

"But family? It's so far away!" Suzie was fishing.

I didn't want to get into family. I am almost an orphan. My father died when I was six and my mother soon after the war.

It was Max Devereux who took me on. He had a full household in Hong Kong, with nannies and staff, where he was working at the time. But friends always seem to have more family than they know what to do with. So, I rather ducked Suzie's probe. But it was prescient.

The next day the hall porter at the club handed me a letter, postmarked Berkshire. Brimming with curiosity, I opened it.

Church Cottage
Childrey, near Wantage Berks SN7 Sl5

My dear nephew,

How jolly to learn you are in England at last! I hope you remember your old auntie. I must see you again and hear all about Singapore and all you are doing. Come for a long weekend. This is not an invitation – it's a command!!!

Take a bus to Wantage via Oxford and then a taxi here. Ask for Edgar at the taxi stand – he knows me well. I don't drive any more or I would meet you.

I have no telephone – my hearing is not what it was.
Looking forward. I suppose you are very tall now.

Your loving auntie,
Ethel Williams
10 September 20…

To say that the receipt of this letter and its contents represented the biggest shock since my arrival in London would be to indulge in understatement. I examined the envelope again. It was certainly addressed to Jonathan Williams, Esq, c/o…Club, St James, etc. I found my friend in the bar.

"I say, Stanton, Suzie was talking about family at that very pleasant dinner last night. Well, look at this." I handed him the letter, which he perused quickly.

"So, you have an aunt who wants to see you – what's strange about that?" He gave me back the letter.

"Plenty – I was certain she had died some years ago. I spent one, maybe two, school holidays with her over twenty years ago. She and my Uncle Max didn't get on at all. I've had no contact with her ever since, and finally – how on earth does she know I'm here?"

"Sounds mysterious. You'll just have to go and see, won't you?"

I could write off the erroneous reference to Singapore as natural after so long a separation. But the tone of the letter seemed odd. I had difficulty imagining the appearance of Aunt Ethel in my mind's eye, but I certainly recalled she was cold and stern, showing little affection for a lonely and motherless child. Curiosity above all prompted me to follow Billy Stanton's advice – certainly not strong family feeling.

The instructions were correct in requiring me to change busses at Oxford for Wantage. There I found the taxi stand and asked for Edgar. A cabbie told me he was not there.

"But where are you headed, Guv?" said my informant. I showed him the address, asking if he knew the way. "Church Cottage's gotta be next to the church, right, Guv? The church has gotta steeple, right? You can see the steeple when you get to the village, right? I'll find it, Guv."

This rural logic impressed me, and we set off. Childrey turned out to be an iconic Berkshire village nestled in the vale, almost at the foot of the hillside with the giant horse, marked out in white chalk by the ancients, which gives the vale its name. And Church Cottage seemed less cottage than small manor house – not large enough to be the original vicarage, now a Victorian house one could spy nearby. But it could have been named the Old Vicarage, so close did it stand to the church. There was a large barn, now accommodating a garage and a flat above. The commodious garden had an area of strawberries covered in netting, hardly necessary at the autumn season. The house itself has covered in wisteria and roses and seemed to carry an excessive number of chimney stacks.

As we drove up, Aunt Ethel – I could only presume it was her – literally stalked from the house with giant steps and enveloped me in a tight embrace. She was dressed in a nubby tweed suit with a silk blouse, thick stockings, and sensible shoes. Her grey hair was wound around her head in plaits; she wore no makeup on a weather-beaten face, other than a touch of pink on the lips. I certainly did not recognise her. She seemed more mannish and even boisterous than I recalled Aunt Ethel, but I kept telling myself that some 25 years had passed since I last saw her.

"Thank you so much for asking me, Aunt Ethel."

"A summons, nephew! A summons – thank you for answering!" And she slapped me on the back.

As I turned to pay the cab, she pushed me aside saying, "No way, no way!" and then to the cabbie, "Where's Edgar?" as she pulled some money out of a jacket pocket.

"Off today, missus," said the cabbie, pulling the brim of his cap.

"Well, tell him not to be off when I have a guest coming!"

As the cab drove off, I began to sense a wonder that was to remain during my stay. I simply could not tie this lady's general manner and even appearance, with my very vague recollections of my time in Tenby. But that very vagueness led me to believe that I was not just witnessing a transformation in my aunt, but really experiencing a major flaw in memory. We often distort our memory and particularly colour in bright shades a time that was, in fact, very dark.

At tea and dinner later that evening, our conversation was an exchange of inaccuracies in recollection, and explanations of sort.

"I live in Hong Kong, not Singapore, Aunt Ethel."

"Oh, yes I forgot, well it's all Chinese – and they eat dogs, don't they?"

"But not pets."

"Don't you believe it, nephew! Anyways, your poor father died in the defence of Singapore, did he not?"

"Actually, his ship was torpedoed off the Borneo coast."

"Well, same thing."

But I was keen to ask questions myself.

"How did you know I was here, Aunt Ethel?"

"Of course, I saw the report of the service for that old goat, Devereux, your guardian – and there was your name. I know I mustn't malign the dead, but we never saw eye to eye, did we? And there was the name of some admiral representing his club – yours as well, I thought. Your auntie may be a good deal older, but she ain't any dimmer, dear nephew!"

I asked about Tenby.

"What a cute little boy you were – and on that coloured pony! (I had no pony). We had some nice times. I was furious when that so-called guardian took you away (I remembered she was relieved). Well, I got fed up with the place when I couldn't have you to stay (*how unlikely*, I thought) so, after some stops here and there, I bought this place."

On the following day, we spent time looking at the garden and the church, and I was told a nice neighbour was coming to dine.

"It's Joan Delavigne, widow of a trainer – madly horsey. She'll invite you to go hacking – you ride, don't you?"

"Yes."

"She'll lend you britches and boots, she has plenty – ex-lovers, I shouldn't wonder – amazing what they leave behind."

I could not imagine my old Aunt Ethel engaging in a speculation of that nature. Of course, she would not have spoken in such an adult manner before a child, but it still seemed out of character.

Lady Delavigne, widow of the baronet trainer Sir George, was charming and somewhat guarded that evening. I placed her as several years younger than my aunt, who she seemed to view with an amused scepticism. Next day we went hacking, I in borrowed jodhpurs, around the lovely Berkshire lanes, with the odd gallop across a meadow. She hunted with the Old Berks and told me tales of famous runs in the environs.

Then she asked, "What do you think of your auntie, after all these years?"

"Frankly, I'm taken aback but of course my memory is so hazy. It was a long time ago, I was very lonely when I stayed with her, and we didn't talk much. If only we had seen each other in recent years, she would be more familiar to me."

"That's if she is your aunt," said Joan, very quietly.

"What?" I pulled up with a jerk on the reins.

"I've shocked you," said Joan Delavigne – she had pulled up as well and was patting the neck of her mount.

"You certainly have!" And we walked on.

"Listen, I've been hoping someone like you would turn up. There is something decidedly queer about Ethel Williams. She turned up here knowing no one and her stories about herself are inconsistent. My elder sister was at the school Ethel claims to have attended – they might not have been there at the same time, but Liz says there is no mention of an Ethel Williams in the school catalogue. Do you know where she went to school?"

"I have no idea! You see, my father hardly mentioned her at home except to say he had been in touch when I went off to school in England. I know so little about her and my father left home as a youngster to go to sea. I don't think he was close to his sister."

"Well, I hate to raise suspicions, but I would do some checking if I were you."

After this exchange, the remainder of my stay with Aunt Ethel was somewhat strained – at least for me. She continued to surprise me, telling stories designed to stress her eccentricities, as when she pulled the emergency cord on a train having seen a sheep cast in a field, and insisted the guard join her in going out to right the animal. At one point, as we sat by the fire, she chucked her bank statements at me and asked me to comment on her shareholdings. I could ascertain a not inconsiderable total value, all in her name at her current address. None of this told me anything.

We parted on Monday with much good cheer on her part, and with Edgar to drive me, plus an insistence I come again before leaving for home. But I was determined to do some detective work and my first move was towards Tommy Devereux, my guardian's son. Fortune placed him in the club bar.

"Tommy! So sorry we couldn't chat at the memorial service – and very well done, it was. Uncle Max would have been more than pleased."

"Terrible crush! Really kind of you to come all this way. Tell me your news – let's go up to lunch and grab a table." I was soon able to begin my enquiry.

"Tommy, do you remember my Aunt Ethel?"

"Very vaguely. I don't think my father was too keen on her. I assume she is no longer with us?"

"Good question – look here, do you suppose there would be any letters or anything of your father's that would indicate whether she died in Tenby or somewhere else?"

"I'll look, but I know who might know off hand – Miss Jones, my father's long-time secretary – you remember her? She was at the service."

"Of course! I should have thought of her – I remember her very well." It was discourteous not to have looked for her, I said to myself.

"Don't worry – I'll ask her – with your compliments!"

It wasn't long before Tommy came back to me. Miss Jones knew for certain that Ethel had left Tenby for a nursing home in Oxford – she had no date for that move, and she was quite certain she had died there as there was a note in her diary for 1st April to remind her to inform me in Hong Kong, which she now realised – to her eternal shame – she had failed to do. Would I ever forgive her? To compound her extraordinary lapse in secretarial duties, she did not have the name of the nursing home.

I was so astounded by this news that I omitted to engage in some comforting contact with Miss Jones or to send flowers or do anything to allay her fears about my presumed displeasure. I thought I would do that later. I began a meticulous search of Oxford nursing homes by telephone and struck gold on the sixth. Yes, a Miss Ethel Williams had been a resident and died on 1st April those few years ago. I decided I needed to talk directly, entrained for Oxford, and was received by the matron in charge.

"You know, Mr Williams," the prim and starched lady intoned, "we had no family contact for your aunt, a lapse we are determined not to repeat, and we now require such before we will admit an applicant. We did have the name of a solicitor who had visited her – the only visitor she ever had, I might say, and we informed him." The matron clearly regarded me as a totally neglectful relative.

Explaining I lived in Hong Kong, a mitigating factor I trusted, I asked what she could tell me about my aunt during her residence.

"Well…" she said, and that single word reeked of disapproval. "Miss Williams formed an attachment with another lady – a somewhat younger inmate. I cannot say who initiated this so-called friendship, but I suspect it was Miss Bumstead. They were never apart, constantly whispering conspiratorially, and upset our other patients with suspicions of what, I know not! All I can say is that it was most improper and, more than once, we considered dismissing them both."

"But what happened to Miss Bumstead?" I asked.

"Well!" and this exclamation was followed by a grunt which sounded like 'humph!' "Miss Williams was hardly cold in her bed when Miss Bumstead departed – with no notice and, we suspected, some of her friend's clothes. We forswore to pursue her, mindful of publicity and our reputation. We had a family contact, but we saw no reason to disturb them."

Leaving the matron's imagination to run its no doubt pleasurable course, I asked for the name of the solicitor.

My next port of call was the musty offices of the bent and pince-nez wearing Mr Abernathy, as indicated by the matron, with a 'much good it will do you' sneer in her voice.

"I wish I had known of you at the time, Mr Williams," he complained, as he drew a dusty file from a dusty cabinet. Clearly Aunt Ethel's business had been insufficient to justify one of the box files which lined several shelves. "You see, I had no point of contact with anyone, and I sorely needed such."

"But can you tell me the nature of your business when you called at the home?" I ventured.

"As she is deceased and you are a relative, I believe I can." And Mr Abernathy carefully drew a document from an otherwise empty file. "I was asked to prepare and certify the signatures on a deed of gift whereby Miss Ethel Williams passed her entire estate, consisting primarily of cash and securities lying at her bankers, to Miss Abigail Bumstead, no conditions of any sort pertaining. You will imagine how I would have welcomed the sanction of some family member. Miss Williams assured me she had none living."

"Can I ask you something else, Mr Abernathy – of course against the submission by you of an appropriate invoice for your honorarium?" I had decided in my excitement to talk lawyer lingo.

"There can be no question of that, Mr Williams. I am honoured by your visit, despite its academic nature regarding my initial charge."

"Is it a criminal offence to assume the identity of a person deceased?"

"Only if such assumption is motivated by, or is in association with a fraudulent purpose which, in turn, is executed resulting in third party loss, or if the false identity is cited within the terms of a commercial transaction specifying the requirement of a true statement of identity as validation, or if given on an application for a driving permit, social security or other benefit or perquisite – and possibly if such assumption of a false identity is harmful to the peace or well-being of a third party, in which case a civil case may be made by the injured party."

Believe it or not, Mr Abernathy delivered this in a tone reminiscent of a liturgical chant – without drawing breath.

As an afterthought, he added: "If you are wondering whether Miss Bumstead has the right to the funds of Miss Williams, should she and any part be still extant, the answer is yes, of course. The deed of gift is entirely regular."

I thanked Mr Abernathy profusely for having sealed my project of detection, On the way back to London, I reviewed in my mind the lengthy legal lesson I had been given gratis. I decided that my 'new' aunt was unlikely to trip over any of the snares listed and my peace had hardly been violated by her deception. On the contrary, this had made not only my day, but my whole visit. But she had taken a bit of a risk in summoning me. No doubt she was lonely in her false shell.

Back in London, I sent flowers to Miss Jones, and I invited myself to dinner at the Stanton's.

"Do I have a story to tell you!" I announced on arrival.

"Is it about your visit to your Aunt Ethel?" asked Billy.

"You bet!"

"Oh goody!" said Suzie. "I just love stories about wicked aunts and uncles – they usually are, aren't they? We had one in the family. An aunt, who my mother disliked intensely – they were on non-speaks. She ended up in a nursing home in Oxford but then she disappeared – poof! In a puff of smoke! Never to be heard of again. Of course, my brother and I loved inventing stories about her: a jail bird, secret agent for MI5, Soviet mole – you know. I imagine she's dead."

"What was her name?" I asked, in my most innocent voice.

"Abigail Bumstead," replied Suzie.

"Well, she's not dead, and I have found her for you." And I told my story.

FINIS

Seventh Tale

The House

The house suited me in every way, as I emphatically explained to the agent who, having completed his promotional patter on the physical attributes of the property, now sought to enlarge his discourse by a tedious account of the previous owners. I cared nothing for tales of the exploitations and greed of the family which had built its fortune on the black backs of tropical slaves, nor was I interested in the dreary details of its fall from grace. My approval of the house as the refuge I sought was based on its desolate location, the number and variety of its rooms and the spaciousness which would allow me to saunter freely, when inclement weather discouraged access to the grounds.

We were in the 'black country', that green and pleasant land now stained with the soot from the devilish furnaces in which man had devised the tools of his own destruction. No greater proof could exist of the nefarious consequences of industrialisation than the blackened verdure and stunted growth of nature's treasures, which covered the countryside like a veil of greasy gossamer. Around my new domicile were other stately residences now empty, but for the echo of past frivolities, parks and fields which had once resounded to the cry of hounds, and now bore the crusted scars of mass residential development. But this environment of civilised decay, so typical of man's twisted urge to foul his own nest, rather suited my literary intentions. I planned to write of decline not achievement, of fall rather than rise, of the end not the beginning. I would relish the solitude of a voluntary imprisonment, surrounded by the spoiled wrapping of yesteryear's gifts, deep within the muddy footprint of a long-lost ramble in time.

The unmade road leading to my new domicile signalled its unique characteristics. The shrubs and patchy grass on either side carried not the fresh and shimmering dew of rosy morn, but – despite the absence of recent rain fall – a sleek humidity, as if the sweat of laboured growth from impoverished soil. The park, which once had held the house in close and warm embrace, now harboured broken oaks, the limbs of which lay scattered, like magical sticks thrown by some girdled gypsy witch. Spider weeds prevailed to smother the remaining patches of lawn. The house itself, of brownish stone held firm by various tenacious vines, was covered by a slate roof of metallic grey, infested by moss, grown beige with age. On entering the hall, through huge oak doors, with rusted key plates and edges frayed by dry rot, one was surprised by frescoes adorning the walls and the vaulted ceiling, criss-crossed with oaken beams. The décor depicted classical themes, nymphs, and satyrs; gods surveyed by a huge Zeus at the apex of the roof, seated on a stormy cloud, and holding bolts of lightning. The artist had planned to sign his work, in a corner of the longest wall, but someone – perhaps the artist himself – had partly covered the signature with what seemed to be an arrogant and angry swipe of the paint brush. Rooms departed *enfilade* to east and west wings. The upper story, reached by a double staircase with elaborately carved bannisters, had been closed off, eliciting abject apologies from the agent but an expression of thankful satisfaction from myself. I had no need of supplementary accommodation.

The first room to the east, no doubt intended for guests waiting to be announced, had walls covered with shells of very type and size which had been fixed in a mass above the chair rail, displaying a pearly hue in the shimmering light, but inciting the clammy feeling of a cold, mussel shell strewn beach in winter. The next room was a library, the walls shelved to hold musty volumes on every subject but with a bias for the occult and the bloody wars of history - I could not but notice. Then came the main drawing room furnished in heavy Victorian pieces, with chairs and sofas covered in worn velvet and stark horsehair. On the walls were hung a collection of nineteenth-century portraits and pictures, depicting scenes of every type – from sweeping landscapes to bucolic village fetes and cluttered townscapes.

And at the end of the wing was a large bedroom, which I intended to make my own, with French windows on three sides, and furnished with an excess of chintz and a contrived femininity – suitable for a Parisian courtesan, perhaps – but strangely out of context in this Midland wilderness. But I hoped to find the peace of contrary isolation and perhaps the vice of lubricious reflection in this odd setting. I had examined the kitchens in the subbasement with their hanging coppers and utensils and wood burning stove. A dumb waiter connected to the dining room above, where the walls were festooned with stuffed heads of game – normally the wall hangings of a great hall – perhaps displaced by the frescoes.

All this was the stuff of my abode, where I planned to embark on a literary project inspired by this new domicile, with an emphasis on decay rather than generation, decline rather than development – as I have already intimated. I fully expected that its location and the air of dissipated lives would lend credence to the theme of my work which I intended for publication, on emerging again in the outside world – a world perhaps unwelcoming, as it was currently struggling with the spread of an oriental virus, and this had prompted a series of public policies designed to flatter the egos of the political class, and the thirst for sensation of the media. I was effortlessly compliant with the myriad restrictions imposed on a gormless and easily cowed public; safe in my self-imposed exile and impatient to exploit its unique features with intellectual and emotional indulgences largely absent in the world outside.

But it was not to be. Like the dreams of rapturous romance of the adolescent, or the lust for avaricious gain by the speculator, my cup of naïve hope was to be dashed to the ground before it touched my lips. My plans were to go awry from the outset – my ambitions crushed by the suddenness of extraordinary events, my reason put at risk, my very soul in mortal danger. A thunderclap announced the horrors which were about to engulf me. I rose from a fitful slumber to cross the rooms to verify that the great front door was secure. But in the hall, I saw, illuminated by flashes of lightening, great blisters on the frescoes, from which emanated some noxious liquid. They were not static, but spreading and increasing, seeming to direct their contamination to the faces and intimate parts of the figures depicted. Their effusions made lines like rivulets of slime descending to the floor. But this was not the limit of the destructive forces released by some evil greater than the storm that raged outside. For then I heard a gnawing noise over the dull din of the rain. A thousand woodworms were consuming the carved oak bannisters, creating lace like patches which then crumbled into sawdust and the faded carpet stairs were already covered in debris. I fled to my room and downed several draughts of whiskey from the carafe in a tantalus.

Morpheus knew me not that night. I tossed and turned, my brain on fire from the images that continued to haunt me. They burnt like the coals that are so fiercer than the first faint flames, the horror of that scene branded forever in my mind. At dreary dawn, I summoned up the courage to return to the hall where I perceived the blisters on the desecrated frescoes now dry and flattened, the floor below strewn with fragments of paint and plaster. I could see no fissure or gaps in the joining of the walls and ceilings which might have allowed the fury of the storm to enter. The bannisters on the stairway were all but destroyed; there remained but a few uprights, like cabbage stalks, and sawdust caked the worn carpets. Returning to my room, I could not bear to revisit this scene of desolation, and now used the French windows of my room for any egress and the backdoor of the kitchen to reach the dining room. My work was made impossible by the woeful wonder at this disaster and its causes. What evil spirit had determined on this visitation, and what was there in my presence or comportment that served as motivation for its monstrous wreckage?

On the following night, I was woken by a sense of some slippery sensation on my skin, as though some unknown essence was pervading its surface – a slithering and alien inkling, not painful but disagreeable. I rose in sodden, semi-slumber and, in bare feet, proceeded to investigate. Reaching the visitors' room, decorated with its walls of pearly shells, I viewed, with terrible trepidation, thousands of snails emerging from their domed shells, slowly – their horned heads turning hither and wither, as if uncertain of destination. As I watched, transfixed with horror, and unable to look down, I conceived my bare feet were resting on a bed of unshelled clams and oysters, soft and slippery, but interspersed with pebble-like bodies which might be pearls. Heedless of the uncertain footing that my mind anticipated, I fled in terror.

This latest phenomenon unnerved me completely and I lay on the satin-draped bed of my room in a dull trance, seeking to revive sufficient reason to move my languid limbs and resort to the clean night air, seeking solace in its restorative powers. I was then able to reach the kitchen and sat huddled and blanketed before the still-glowing ashes of the stove.

When morning's ruddy glow appeared, I returned and with faltering steps, ventured to view the visitors' room. I found little if any sign of the heinous apparitions of the night. A few shells had been loosened from their applications to the wall and lay on the floor. Otherwise, the room seemed undisturbed. This did nothing to cauterise the gaping wound in my consciousness. On the contrary, I began to suspect an attack of malignant mania brought on by I knew not what external forces, or some insidious transformation of my own psyche. I paced the weed-infested lawn in agonised deliberation, and turned to view the house, which seemed to return my stare with mocking derision and hypocritical calm.

The next night brought no relief, but further, horrific manifestations, confirming incipient madness on my part, or the inexplicable occurrence of unnatural forces embedded in the house itself. I heard distant voices, not emanating from outside, but with the resonance that accompanies conversations in an adjoining room. I could not bear to lay still, even though the palpitations of my heart threatened to break through my reverberating rib cage. The voices grew louder, and as I touched the light-switch, I could observe that the persons depicted in the paintings on the wall were talking – conversing, their lips moving and their faces expressing the tenor of their dialogue. The portraits spoke directly to me, their eyes boring into mine. I could not decipher their words. They resembled the careless chatter one hears in a crowded room – the language is recognisable, but the words are indistinct with only a slight hint of meaning. But the murmuring of human voices was underscored by the sounds of nature emanating from the unpopulated landscapes and clamour of the cities and towns represented. It was as though the paintings had been transformed into films made by fixed cameras – the rippling streams gurgled, the waving wheat whispered, the town streets echoed with the blare of municipal mechanisms. The room was alive, churning with life and activity. I stood transfixed with horror and consternation but now convinced that I could no longer bear the wretched repugnance of everything associated with the house.

Again, I repaired to my room and whiskey decanter, and then to the kitchen through the service door, reviving the woodstove fire, and passing the remainder of the dark night in a chair. I was startled from my despondent doze by a noise similar to the one I had heard in the hall on that first night of terror. It was best described as munching, as cows chewing their cud, or even dogs gnawing a bone. I rose and passed through the dining room to glimpse the hall. A wriggling mass of woodworm had begun on the oaked beams of the ceiling, and I did not stay to monitor their progress. I rushed to my room, threw this folio and some necessities into a case, and fled to the neglected park which lay before the house. A rumbling noise grew in intensity, and I turned to look once more at the house – its dank features cloaked in morning mist. And then I stood and watched as a collapse, agonising in its slowness, began in the West Wing. Like a deck of playing cards, the edifice began to shudder in waves. Tumbling stones and fracturing roof slates were imploding in slow motion, creating disparate ridges of rubble, moving from west to east, dust exploding into grey and greasy clouds, the roar of disintegration increasing in volume, until at the end, a stillness fell upon the wreckage, and I thought I could hear faint and muffled cries, of whom or what, my fevered brain refused to speculate upon. The house was gone – my reason with it.

Post Scriptum

This account, folded in a leather folio, was found by a shepherd, next to a pile of soiled and dusty clothing, on the edge of a cliff, looking out to sea. The still unidentified author, and presumably owner of the clothing, had thrown himself, naked, on to the rocks below. The recovery of his body posed considerable difficulty, and identification is still pending.
Angus McClintock, Cumberland Constabulary

FINIS

Eighth Tale

The Pianist

Joe Ventri closed the lid on his piano keyboard, and lit his first cigarette of the evening, as he listlessly watched his bassist and drummer packing up. They could do it in their sleep, he reckoned. He felt particularly for Ben, and all drummers, for that matter. How fortunate to have ended his musical apprenticeship on the piano – no instrument to pack and carry. Bill had his bass fiddle to lug around. What was that movie that had Hitchcock boarding a train with a bass fiddle case? He always insisted on a brief appearance in his films – a sort of 'spot the director' game.

In his mind's ear, Joe could still hear the last bars of his signature, sign-off tune, *Bye Bye, Blackbird*. He ended it with a left-hand cord, repeated in double time – in the style of Errol Garner, and Ben began a drumroll to back it. By now he had forgotten why he chose that number, but he liked to sing the lyric to the remains of the after-theatre crowd at midnight in the Peacock Lounge, where the *Joe Ventri Trio* was a permanent attraction.

Pack up all my cares and woes,
Here I go – singing low, Bye, Bye Blackbird.
Where somebody waits for me,
Sugar's sweet and so is she,
Bye, Bye Blackbird

Perhaps it was at a moment like this – watching his colleagues pack up – that gave him the idea. Almost everything in life, whether it be a physical or emotional event, reminded Joe of a song. They buzzed in his head as a soothing background, as the Muzak in the elevator is supposed to do but fails through surfeit. Joe would never tire of his repeating themes from the American Song

Book. The length and breadth of his repertoire had been a major selling point in his first meeting and audition with the management of the Carlyle Hotel. His party trick, so to speak, was imitations of the style of famous pianists, and this was the basis of the show, staged twice in the evening at nine and eleven. The lights would dim, a spot on the piano switched on, and the well-spoken headwaiter would take the mike and announce: "Ladies and gentlemen, the Peacock Lounge has the honour to present the great Joe Ventri!"

Joe had tried to eliminate the 'great' from this introduction which he considered 'over the top' but, management had explained that the Carlyle Hotel only engaged 'great artists' and he was lucky to be among those so honoured by a 'great' hotel. As they were paying him $250 a week, he demurred. And his turn consisted of imitating all the real 'greats': Errol Garner, Fats Waller, Bill Evans, Dave Brubeck, Thelonious Monk, Count Basie, Nat King Cole, Oscar Peterson (although he couldn't match the speed of Oscar's fingering), George Shearing, and even Jacques Lousier and his swinging renditions of Bach. Where appropriate, Joe sang along and his imitation of Nat King Cole's unique singing style in *Autumn Leaves* drew immediate applause. In between his turns, Joe and his rhythm section tinkled away on his extensive repertoire, deftly handling requests brought to him by waiters, or the customers themselves.

Joe Ventri was born to Giovanni Ventrini in the Little Italy section of New York City. When a professional career had beckoned, Joe had thought first of changing his name to Johnny Ventri but had decided that Joe sounded 'catchier'. His was a musical family, his father had hoped for a career as a violin soloist but had finally settled – in his frustrated estimation – for a mundane job in the string section of the New York Philharmonic, where he could also fill in on viola. Joe's Irish mother had a pleasant, church-choir voice and was sufficiently self-trained to give lessons to children in the neighbourhood. The family budget had included both violin and piano lessons for young Giovanni, but the piano had come to dominate early on. Growing up in the very ethnically focussed neighbourhood, Joe's playmates were mostly bilingual Italians and Elizaveta – daughter of a former musician, now owner of a trattoria on Lower Broadway – was a family favourite. When the innocent and childish affection of these two playmates suffered an amorous transformation, brought on by adolescent urges – at least on Joe's part – it became increasingly obvious that only marriage should ensure its proper consummation. Joe's father had managed to secure a scholarship at Julliard for his talented son through his contacts at the Philharmonic. This should have delayed the hymeneal occasion, but as needs must, Liza and Joe were married (far too early, family friends said) at the age of 19. For three years, they lived under a parental roof, until Joe started to get some evening gigs. While continuing his classical formation at Julliard, he had moved increasingly toward the jazz medium, and he and Liza spent evenings at Manhattan jazz clubs, with Joe even standing it at times for the regular pianist at Eddie Condon's. He joined the musician's union and got his first job in a midtown cocktail bar, where his hours were six to ten. As Joe's career progressed – on the cocktail bar circuit, but then for private parties and with touring big bands and small groups – his work was increasingly focussed on the nocturnal hours. Liza had entertained some ambition as a professional singer, encouraged by her mother-in-law, dreaming even of joining Joe as a chanteuse in nightclub gigs, but her enthusiasm waned, and she found a good job with a music publisher – also based on Lower Broadway. This allowed her the opportunity of helping her father at the trattoria at lunch and in the evening. Thus, she told friends they were a three-job family – as she certainly kept her tips.

But the pattern of work of the young Ventri family not only dissuaded any inclination to have children – much to the dismay of their very Catholic parents – but began to put a strain on the marriage itself. Joe was working almost exclusively at night, requiring sleep through to midday, and Liza rose early for her job at the office, working until nine or ten on many evenings at the trattoria. But that latter supplementary occupation brought further opportunities for discord and heartbreak. The trattoria was a favourite watering spot for young bucks from Wall Street, always on the lookout for lunchtime flirtations that might lead to further extracurricular activity. Liza was more than a comely lass; she was a highly seductive beauty with a warm nature to match and a deficit in male company, given the mismatch in the couples' working hours. A first, offhand affair with a Wall Street stockbroker led to another, and then to a pattern of promiscuous infidelity.

At first, Joe was not aware of this blatant non-compliance with his spouse's marriage vows, until his father-in-law took him aside to say he no longer wished to have his daughter helping in the restaurant, as he was shocked by her flirtatious behaviour, and suggested Joe better look to his wife – in words loaded with meaning. After considerable reflection, Joe was almost surprised to find he suffered no physical jealousy nor even a sense of injury to his pride – perhaps because on some tours with a band to cities across the nation, he had sinned in this respect himself. Of course, divorce was out of the question – this being at least one Catholic principle he was willing to endorse fully – its economic benefit in the saving of lawyer's fees being incontestable. The couple found time to have a heart-to-heart discussion, which ended in both agreeing that an open marriage suited their circumstances perfectly, saved family face, and preserved that mutual affection that had bound them since they had romped together as childhood playmates.

Joe celebrated this new, felicitous condition by adding to his turn, a highly ironic rendition of the infamous classic:

Love and marriage, love and marriage, go together like a horse and carriage!

The Peacock Lounge, as one of New York's leading nightspots, had a regular clientele, and one prominent figure was a three-times married and highly glamorous heiress who kept a suite in the hotel for her frequent sojourns away from her vast Long Island estate. She was Hilda van Ness, and she professed a deep love for jazz, the passion with which she entirely justified the seduction of her favourite pianist, Joe Ventri. She set about this with the dedication and industry, which had doubtless seeded the great shipping fortune of her ancestor. An accomplished amateur singer herself, she had adopted the style of Anita O'Day, and persuaded the management to allow her to sing a number with the Joe Ventri Trio. This required the consent of the musician's union which was easily secured by a sizeable contribution to the union's pension fund from the van Ness coffers. Her signature number was *A Nightingale Sang in Berkeley Square*:

That certain night,
The night we met,
There was magic abroad in the air,
There were angels dining at the Ritz,
And a nightingale sang in Berkeley Square.

Hilda sang the first few bars sotto voce, mike in hand, leaning over the piano – as if addressing Joe, who was touching the accompanying chords.

I may be right, I may be wrong,
But I'm perfectly willing to swear.
That when you turned and smiled at me,
A nightingale sang in Berkeley Square.

Then she began to swing it up-tempo, left ten bars of refrain for Joe to improvise, and then ended with a scat rendition, *à la* divine Ella. The public roared their approval and Joe was ensnared – a musical seduction he could not resist. Their affair progressed at breakneck speed, with great ease of encounter, due to Hilda's suite on the 33rd floor, and the Oyster Bay estate for weekends.

On these occasions, Joe found himself mixing with the Social Register set, and he soon realised that Hilda could not be written off as a sexual predator whose appetite would be satisfied with a short-term performance. Her seductive instincts were also social, and she sought to inculcate Joe as a permanent feature in her lazy life – finding him susceptible to the necessary acclimatisation as a member of her class. In fact, the job was half done. Joe was good-looking in a well-groomed and distinguished way – he dressed in a conservative style he had copied through his interaction with the patrons of the Carlyle Hotel. He spoke well, and his talent as a mimic facilitated the adoption of a 'Locust Valley Lockjaw' accent. The only thing missing, Hilda soon realised, was a sense of commitment. Joe didn't seem comfortable with the role of a kept man – a pet to supplement her hobby of jazz singing. To try to distress the contamination that Joe's professional status might lend to his social standing, she wished him not to play for her guests, but rather to mingle on an equal footing. But to strengthen her growing grasp on his affections, she also cast herself as a quasi-professional partner, financing a recording and producing a disk entitled *Hilda van Ness Sings with the Joe Verdi Trio*. This achieved a certain circulation, having attracted the attention of the society columnists, and became a popular Christmas gift. But the notoriety resulting from this initiative fuelled a nagging doubt in Joe's mind about the direction in which this affair might be going.

Cholly Knickerbocker, 'Society's favourite gossip columnist' (really Emma Goldfarb from the Bronx), wrote:

"The 'in' crowd are wondering when nuptial delight might crown the ongoing tryst between shipping heiress Hilda van Ness and Peacock Lounge keyboard thumper Joe Ventri. Wavy-haired heartthrob Joe seems to spend all his

leisure moments with jazz-loving Hilda, who I am told has staked him out to be her fourth. Expect a swinging Wedding March in Oyster Bay."

This report annoyed Joe mildly, sent Liza into fits of giggles over the 'wavy-haired heartthrob' phrase, and sent Hilda into a rage – the one person who should have been accustomed to such press coverage. The management of the Carlyle was always happy with any publicity associating them with high society and gave Joe a pat on the back. But unwelcome publicity festers like a wound to the sensitive psyche and both Hilda and Joe paused and took a deep breath to relieve that tightness in the chest that heartaches produce. Finally, Joe, in a quiet moment on the 33rd floor, sat Hilda down with a cognac in hand, and said they must have a quiet talk. But Joe said, "I have to sing it!" He sat down at the photograph-laden Steinway that graced Hilda's suite and began:

It was just one of those things.
Just one of those crazy flings.
One of those bells than now and then rings. Just one of those things.

Joe nodded to Hilda, who was leaning on the piano, and she took up the next stanza of the refrain:

It was just one of those nights,
Just one of those fabulous flights, A trip to the moon on gossamer wings, just one of those things.

Then Joe again for the bridge – or the middle, as it is sometimes called.

If we'd thought a bit before the end of it, when we started painting the town.
We'd have been aware that our love affair, was too hot, not to cool down,

Then, the two lovers sang the last stanza in tight harmony:

So goodbye Dear, and amen,
Here's hoping we meet now and then.
It was great fun,
But it was just one of those things.

They clasped in a passionate kiss, and Joe took the elevator down and a taxi home.

Naturally Cholly Knickerbocker did not admit he had been premature in his column – journalists don't retract without litigation and injunctions. Joe carried on and found welcome evidence of his reluctant notoriety in the enthusiasm of his audience. The management had introduced a reservation only policy. One of its most faithful customers was a demure young lady, usually escorted by a feckless-looking youth. It hadn't taken Joe long to discover from the headwaiter that she was Abagail Adams. "Southampton – new money." He had sniffed.

Abagail was particularly persistent in her requests from Joe's repertoire, which she delivered personally, hanging over the piano and closing her eyes as he played her request. *At least she doesn't sing*, thought Joe. But she was charming, he admitted alarmingly. A fresh, babyish face, a hairstyle suitable to her age, a well-turned, somewhat athletic figure, an aura of freshness and only recently diluted innocence – all combined to ignite Joe's libidinous curiosity – further supported by the striking contrast between this girl and his recently separated paramour. One night, Joe began to sing her request, which he never normally did until his act was announced:

I've got you under my skin,
I've got you deep in the heart of me,
So deep in my heart that you're really a part of me,
I've got you under my skin.

At this point, Abagail opened her large brown eyes and bored her gaze longingly into Joe's, who continued, his breath shortening a bit.

I've tried so not to give in
I've said to myself this affair will never go so well. But why should I try to
resist when, Baby, I know so well, I've got you under my skin.

These encounters continued for some time until finally, Joe found her at his side when the band was packing up and she whispered in his ear, "Take me home!" How she had shed her escort for the evening, he had not noticed. Perhaps she had left and come back. In any case, she took him to a swish Park Avenue

71

condominium apartment and impressed him with a degree of erotic education she could hardly have acquired at her alma mater Vassar – or perhaps she had, they took boys now. As their affair progressed, it became clear that Abagail had no intention of incorporating Joe into her social circle. She refused to invite him home to Southampton, saying her father was a bore, and she hated her stepmother. On the contrary, Abagail's interest seemed to be in slumming. She took a one-bedroom apartment in a gentrified Bowery loft for their trysts and liked to take him to supper at an all-night eatery - Hamburger Heaven on Madison Avenue, usually populated at one in the morning by taxi drivers and hungry nightclubbers. At weekends, they would escape to Coney Island, or seedy resorts in the Catskills. Abagail liked to intersperse their sessions of strenuous lovemaking with readings from the works of Marcel Proust and Franz Kafka. She clearly longed for the Bohemian life and saw Joe as a window on another world – her upbringing having denied her access.

But even this apparently discreet romantic interlude could not escape the consequences of Joe's cafe society fame. Cholly Knickerbocker wrote again:

"My moles at the Carlyle tell me that Joe Ventri's trio continues to pack in the punters at the Peacock Lounge and it's become standing room only. Joe's been charming New York's 400 and hangers on for three years now – the longest gig in the history of that fashionable night spot. But they also tell me that handsome Joe's favourite afterhours handmaiden is the pert Abigail Adams, whose coming-out party last summer knocked the socks off Southampton's high society. Abigail's pater, media tycoon Bob Adams, stunned the Street this year with his cheeky takeover of Talk Broadcasting. Seems Joe is able to line his piano with mink again, after losing Hilda van Ness to a Gstaad ski instructor."

Once again, Joe got a pat on the back from the management for this plug, but was particularly annoyed by the accompanying comment, "Keep up the good work," which he took to refer to his amorous adventures, rather than his music. It also became clear that this notoriety did not accord with Abigail's concept of slumming, and after a decent interval – not celebrated in song this time – she left him for a Little Neck clam digger, married, and moved to Weekapaug Beach in Rhode Island.

Joe carried on for a bit, but one day his agent called him, and changed his life – something agents do only very infrequently. But now a fabulous career window opened. Joe gave notice to the Carlyle, and his agent soon found a replacement at the Peacock Lounge. He decided to surprise Liza, whose own comportment had undergone reform – so often caused by the boredom of transgressions rather than true repentance. Joe returned home at five o'clock in the afternoon to an astonished Liza, poured her a glass of Chianti, beckoned her to a chair, and informed her that his agent had secured a multi disc recording contract for the Joe Ventri Trio from Columbia, and he would now work only in the morning and relax between recording sessions. He then sat down at their upright piano and sang her this number (a Harry Warren and Mack Gordon standard), somewhat edited:

There will be many other nights like this.
And I'll be sitting here alone with you
There will be other songs to sing,
Another fall, another spring
But there will never be another you.

Joe riffed a few chords as he could see tears welling up in Liza's dark eyes, then continued:

They'll be no other lips for me to kiss,
Cause they won't thrill me like yours will do
Yes, I may dream a million dreams
But now I know they'll all come true
For now, I know there'll never be another you.

Liza got up, her face wet with tears, and quietly led Joe to the bedroom.

FINIS

Ninth Tale
The Vicar

Donald Tressinger was a beneficed clergyman of the Church of England whose appearance, demeanour, personality, education, theological convictions, and career path was entirely unexceptional. If a critic, or even a casual observer, had insisted on identifying some distinguishing feature that marked him out amongst his clerical brethren, it would have been his love of field sports. His joy in non-liturgical life was the walk-up shooting he pursued – together with carefully selected friends, on the 30 acres of glebe attached to the living. He took his annual holiday in early September, accompanied by a pair of spaniels, picking up on the Scottish grouse moors – a welcome guest of more than one laird, who always allowed him a turn in the butts on the last day. He was a car follower of the local hunt and would have ridden to hounds, were it not for the disapproval of his bishop, a position which the Reverend Mr Tressinger considered quite unreasonable – and, indeed, in conformity with no canon law he knew of. Were not hunting parsons quite common in the nineteenth century? As if in defiance, Mr Tressinger, surrounded by a small clutch of High Church supporters, had been observed blessing the hounds at the opening meet, with appropriate references to St Hubert, the patron Saint of hunting, whose name-day is fortuitously in early November.

But Donald Tressinger was not particularly High Church himself. In most things, he considered himself to be middle of the road. The only blot on his standing in the Cotswold village of Luckbury, where he had been vicar for 15 years, was the fact that he had sent parcels to German Lutheran pastors during the war. Notwithstanding that these correspondents were totally anti-Nazi regime, some villagers had taken askance. But otherwise, Donald was much loved, even if he was a bit of a dog snob. The village of Luckbury itself was almost excessively picturesque, with a chalk stream snaking through its stone buildings and standard landmarks. There was a part Saxon church, an Elizabethan stately home, several wool merchant's manor houses, a proliferation of cosy cottages, a coaching inn, several pubs, a village store/post office – even a resident village constable. The population included a cast of characters from an Agatha Christie novel. There was a retired Colonel of Artillery, who chaired the Parish Council, a doctor, a retired professor, two or three maiden aunts, an eccentric, an alcoholic retired actor, two city types and a predatory divorcé.

This combination of iconic features was brought to the attention of a location scout at Pinewood Studios, who was assigned to a film project, based on a saccharine bestseller about a rag-to-riches belle. In fact, the film was a vehicle for a busty star, who had reached the apex of her career, and was clinging to the last remnants of fame before descending to the relative obscurity of guest appearances on TV documentaries for film buffs. The producer/director accompanied a location manager on his second visit to Luckbury and invited the squire to lunch at the old coaching inn, now cunningly renamed *The Fox's Lair* by the new country inn chain who had recently acquired it. This nomenclature disgusted the vicar, who pointed out foxes have earths, not lairs.

"Let me put you right in the frame, Sir Percy," said the wisely named Mr Morecombe, "we'll need a week's shooting down here, and we're talking a five-figure location charge, with full insurance from our completion insurers, day rates for extras from the village, also for assistant grips. We handle the catering – I'm talking to the folks here about accommodation. We set up a small and tidy location village in the meadow behind the church – extra moolah for the padre and church funds. I'll talk to your copper here about security, noise level is minimal. If you like, I can get our accounts chappie to give you a rough estimate of the amount of lucre we're going to be spreading in your village here."

"Er…yes, Mr Morecombe," said the squire, frowning slightly. "I am somewhat familiar with these filmmaking visitations. My good friend, Lord Britches at Pettwold in the Beaufort country, suffered one last year. Ahem…if you will permit me to use that term."

"Wasn't that for 'The Gang's All Here'?" asked Watkins, the location manager.

"Yes…and…" The squire was interrupted.

"That was a two-bit B movie," exclaimed Morecombe. "We're talking top production values here!"

"Of course! I did not imagine the two cases were comparable." Sir Percy was apologetic. "I shall have to consult the parish council. I don't own the whole village, you understand."

"You bet – kick off your pitch with 30,000 smackers!" said Morecombe with a leer.

"Might I not rather say fifty thousand – the disruption, you know…"

"Make it forty."

"Done!" said the squire.

Sir Percy did not bother to clarify that he owned most of the village, and the parish council would have agreed to a visitation from the very devil himself – if the money was right. The vicar was surprised but pleased to hear that the scenes to be shot were mainly a funeral and a wedding, which topped and tailed the plot, and so the church would have a central role in the proceedings.

Some weeks went by whilst the village digested the implications of this historic event and petitioned the vicar for places in church for the critical scenes. Eventually the location manager returned with an assistant casting director – an American – who intrigued a large gathering of the village with his style of address:

"OK, you guys – listen up!" He was standing on a bottle case in the garden of the pub. "We'll be paying ten quid a day for the extras, and fifteen for the assistant grips – that's the guys who tote the equipment. We're asking the vicar, the military guy and one of the ladies in the village to act as stand-ins for the actors playing those roles. That's for back shots, and any later re-shooting we might need. We're casting actors who are as close to these doubles as possible. The stars in the leading roles are bringing their own stand-ins. For the rest of you nice folks, Judy here will take names and numbers of those willing to work – can't promise to use you all."

Meanwhile, the location manager, with a photographer in tow, was taking what he termed 'headshots' of Colonel de Vere, Donald Tressinger and the three maiden ladies – the Misses Tolliver, Bancroft and Jones, the three ladies happily entered into a friendly discussion – in the true spirit of the village.

"I'm sure they won't find an actress that has my ordinary looks," said Miss Tolliver.

"Nonsense! They must all be good-looking, so they're bound to have a match for you, dear Ethel," said Miss Bancroft.

"I'm not at all sure I would like to meet my double," said Miss Jones.

Finally, the day arrived for shooting to begin, and all were taken aback by the number of people involved. The meadow behind the church was filled with lorries, trailers, power units, tents and sundry equipment and the vicar kept asking for assurance that the turf would be restored. Sir Percy comforted him by reminding him how quickly such remedial action was accomplished after the meadow had been used for parking at the hunt ball. But the vicar certainly enjoyed the entire undertaking, even though he found the script he had been given lacking in dramatic quality.

Colonel de Vere struggled to contain his desire to give orders to correct what he deemed to be a most ill-disciplined execution of the process. Still, he obeyed the orders to 'stand there', or 'sit there' with a promptitude that impressed the assistant director. An actress named Betty Bates had been found for the role of the heroine's auntie, and she had more than a passing resemblance to Miss Jones – after hairstyles had been adjusted, and the Misses Tolliver and Bancroft were quite happy as extras in the church congregation. The actor playing a military role had a limp, which amused Colonel de Vere, but the play vicar, with a wig, was a good match of the Reverend Tressinger.

When it was all over, there hung over the village a sense of disappointment, tempered with the pleasurable memory of an experience which could be a subject of pub talk for years. There was only the briefest discussion over the sharing of the forty thousand pounds, with church funds amply enhanced, and no one could complain that the visiting filmmakers had not been openhanded with tips and sundry expenditures.

But the bright sky of recollection was soon darkened by clouds of deep tragedy. One rainy morning, the body of Miss Jones was found on a gravel path in her garden. She had been shot, almost point blank by a shotgun. There were no signs of a break-in or robbery, although her motor car was missing. The vicar was asked to make the formal identification of her body – there being no known family.

At this sad ceremony, Detective Inspector Grogan of Cirencester CID was impressed with Mr Tressinger's calm and lack of squeamishness.

"As you can see, the shotgun must have been held a few feet away – but the face is not entirely disfigured, and the police surgeon thinks it strange that she was apparently not killed instantly. But an autopsy will tell us more."

"Are there signs of shot pellets in the bushes or foliage behind?" asked Donald Tressinger.

"There are not – and I know what you're thinking. Was she killed somewhere else, and the body dumped there? And no one heard the shot! Unfortunately, the rain has washed away visible footprints in the gravel."

Tressinger was looking closely at the body, and even moved the head to one side.

"You won't find a motive in the village," he said. "She was universally loved."

"And it's not a burglary gone wrong – we can't find anything obviously missing – except her car," said the DI.

"I suggest you do a careful search of the house and look into Miss Jones' background. You see, although she's been here a good ten years, we knew nothing of her background. She was discretion itself, never talked about her past or family. We may find clues as to motive in the house. She was very popular with all the film people, but she may have said something to one of them which could be helpful."

DI Grogan was amused at the 'we'. Clearly the vicar had joined the investigation. Unlike the police in G.K. Chesterton's Father Brown stories. Grogan was delighted and promised to keep the vicar closely informed.

A few weeks later, during which time the vicar had tried to comfort villagers, still shocked by an unsolved murder in their midst, DI Grogan turned up at the Vicarage.

"Well, Vicar, I imagine you have been thinking while I have been running around like a lunatic. Not sure where to start. First, the coroner reports death by poison, some time before the shot gun wounds, so the murderer was trying to avoid ID, which is ridiculous. Why dump the body at the victim's house? Next interviews here and there confirm: Miss Jones had no enemies here and doesn't seem to have made any in the film crew. I've talked to the director, location manager and others – none of them knew her before and everybody liked her. The only one I couldn't reach is Betty Bates, who played the auntie – and so Miss Jones was her double. She's gone off to Canada for a TV role – but everyone says they got on very well. They were mostly together during the shooting. So, we are nowhere on motive. The search of the house revealed the only thing that might be missing is Miss Jones' passport. Bank says she had no safe deposit box, so it wasn't there – but she had a valid one – checked with Immigration. Of course, if the murderer was Betty Bates, she might have used it for a getaway – since they looked alike. But where's her motive? We have found the car in a street in West Kensington but no local connection and no one can tell us how long it's been there. Now Miss Jones' private life. Interesting! Very interesting! Regular withdrawals of several hundred pounds every couple of weeks over the last nine months. And neighbours tell us, Miss Jones had taken to going up to London much more frequently. Difficult to fix dates, but the top shop, where she is a regular, pinpoints some more recent ones and they do coincide somewhat with the withdrawals of cash. Now in my experience, that's got all the signs of blackmail, but when does a blackmailer kill his victim – except maybe in a fit of rage? But this is clearly premeditated. If it is blackmail, we'll never know why because we can't find anything in Miss Jones' history. Anyway, if you're wondering about a funeral – we can't release her body yet – it's in the county morgue."

"Tell me, Detective Inspector Grogan. When was Miss Jones' last trip to London?" asked the vicar.

"Two days before the murder, and someone heard the car come back the night of the murder, but no one checked to see if it was Miss Jones and no one heard the murderer drive away, and we now know he didn't use the shotgun in the garden."

"And when was Betty Bates' agent informed of her departure for Canada?"

"Is that relevant? Well, some time before – when the film was finished."

"By a typed and signed note?"

"Yes."

"Was there anything in Miss Jones' house from Betty Bates – a letter perhaps?"

"There was a fresh copy of the screenplay, dedicated to Miss Jones and signed but no letter."

The vicar paused and stroked his chin.

"The body in the morgue," he asked quietly, "is she virgin intacta?"

"No," said the DI, somewhat surprised. "That's checked automatically at the autopsy – but there is no sign of rape."

"That wasn't my concern," said the vicar. "Now about the history of Miss Jones, was her passport renewed recently?"

"Yes, five years ago."

"Get a hold of the renewal form – you'll find one is required to give any former name one was previously known by. I'll wager Miss Jones changed her name. Put the former one up on your police blotter and you'll find a record and fingerprints. Check them against the body and they won't match. Then see what the 'former name' has a record for. I'll bet its murder – but with no conviction. I'll also bet she was accused of murdering her husband. I will further wager that a family member, or close friend, withheld a critical piece of evidence, frustrating the conviction – in order to set the accused up for blackmail – and he stalked her – even though she got her name changed, or perhaps recognised her somewhere."

DI Grogan was open mouthed with admiration.

"But there is still the question of why the blackmailer murdered his milk cow?" asked the confused policeman. "We know she was paying him off. And even if he did murder her in a rage because on her last trip she said, 'no more', why did he dump the body at her house? Why did he want her identified?"

"My dear Detective Inspector Grogan, prepare yourself for a shock!" The vicar had a broad smile – perhaps inappropriate in view of the subject matter. "The blackmailer did not murder Miss Jones. She murdered herself."

"What?"

"At the very beginning, when I viewed the body, I suspected something," continued the vicar. "The lady had pierced ears – I was almost certain Miss Jones did not."

"But then whose body is that in the morgue?" asked a dumbfounded Grogan.

"That's easy. It's Betty Bates. I was almost sure but needed the story you have pieced together with solid detective work. You see, the partial disfigurement with the shotgun exploited a human tendency. When the most important identity clue is not altogether certain, the mind rushes to all supporting evidence. In this case it was the clothes, the hairstyle and the location that made us certain it was Miss Jones."

"But…what? Why?" The Detective Inspector stammered.

"Again, your facts confirm it all. We know that Miss Jones had been paying off the blackmailer regularly, and it stands to reason she had become fed up. With a murder already under her belt, so to speak, an obvious choice was to murder the blackmailer. But might she not be caught? They would find out who had been paying him. Then she met the actress Betty Bates, a look-a-like! And Miss Jones had an inspiration. A novel way to get rid of a blackmailer. She would murder Betty, arrange things so that everyone would think she was the victim, and disappear with another assumed name, leaving the blackmailer behind without a victim. She first forged Betty's signature on a letter she typed for the agent (check the machine in her house). So, no one would miss Betty for a good while. She then went up to London having arranged to meet Betty (who reckoned her a good friend from the shoot) and managed to slip her cyanide."

"In coffee, according to the autopsy," the DI interjected.

"She put the body in her car and drove out to some country lane and shot it with a shotgun, being careful not to totally obliterate the face. You'll find the shotgun…"

"Already have, in the abandoned car – no prints." the DI interposed again.

"She wiped them clean. Then she drove home, dressed the body in her own clothes, rings and so on, arranged the hair appropriately and dumped it on the gravel path in the garden. It was now very late, and when she got back into her car, with her passport, and drove away, no one was likely to hear her. In London, she abandoned the car and took a train to Heathrow where she caught a flight for somewhere – you'll find her name on a passenger list – I guess, Canada. But of course, you never checked this, because her body was lying in the morgue or so she expected us to think. At her destination, she will change her name again. She undoubtedly has funds secreted somewhere. She's been planning an escape from the blackmailer for some time, I shouldn't be surprised."

"But Vicar," said Detective Inspector Grogan, with a somewhat hoarse voice, "if you had mentioned this at the beginning, we might have caught her!"

"I doubt it, Detective Inspector, she was probably already airborne when we were viewing the body. And would you have believed me, without all that you have found out? The blackmailing and so forth? I don't know whether I believed myself. No…you found the pieces of the puzzle and I have merely assembled them."

None of this extraordinary account leaked in the village, because the vicar waited for the police to complete their investigation. They quickly found the record of the murder trial and acquittal of the accused under her then name. Miss Jones was found to have booked and taken a flight to Canada on the day the body of Betty Bates was discovered. A description was flashed, and the Royal Canadian Mounted Police located her easily – she was preparing to live under an assumed name. Extradited back to the UK, Miss Jones pleaded guilty to murder in the first degree, and revealed the name of the blackmailer. He gave up the evidence he had been holding of Miss Jones's first murder, but the Crown Prosecution Service decided not to bother with an additional charge. For the murder of Betty Bates, Miss Jones was sentenced to life imprisonment – to serve a minimum of twenty years. The blackmailer, sentenced to five years, died in a prison brawl after two.

Mr Morecambe's film, entitled *From Riches to Rags* was released to mediocre reviews ("very dull 'aga saga' but with nice location scenes," said one reviewer). Everyone in Luckbury, from Sir Percy down to the last man at the end of the pub bar, considers that the story of Miss Jones and the brilliant detection by their very own vicar, the Reverend Donald Tressinger, would make a far better motion picture.

FINIS

Tenth Tale

The Dealmaker

I had a friend who lived to put deals together. I'll call him Reginald or Reggie, as he preferred. His deals, however, were not of the ordinary kind – these are undertaken by the mundane community of banks and brokers whose business it is to originate and execute financial transactions. Reggie's deals were almost always impossible, eccentric, fanciful, arcane, unlikely, exotic, extreme, more than doubtful, and sometimes downright illegal. These proposed transactions were not simply the natural rejects from the established dealmakers, or from a surplus that had fallen off the table of some well-endowed merchant bank, unable to handle all the business thrown its way. They almost seemed to be sheer inventions, spun from Reggie's inexhaustible horde of hopeful deal completions – designed to astound the traditional banking world with their acrobatic and innovative technique. He didn't just yearn to do a deal – he wanted to cock a snoop at the establishment.

"Look, Mr Morgan, or Mr Rothschild, or Mr Lazard – look at the deal I have done! You would have been too dumb to even consider it!"

This was the dream that drove Reggie to pursue the pot of gold, and the recognition, that lay at the end of his financial rainbow. But inherent in this obsession was the fatal flaw that scars the gambler's sheen of romance. Losses drive the vicious urge even more than gains. That helpless hope of recovery powers the arm that stretches to put one more chip on this or that number, red or black – one more spin of the wheel might find the gaudy gaze of Lady Luck. Reggie found inspiration in failure, invigoration in frustration, optimism in defeat.

I had known Reggie since university days where we belonged to the same club. He had shown no inclination towards high finance at the time – nor had I. He was not a gambler and never joined the all-night poker sessions that I frequented. Reggie hailed from an old and distinguished Southern family, who still maintained their ancestral plantation in a rundown but nostalgic condition. There was nothing in this background that pointed to any career orientation. In those palmy days, we didn't exchange ambitions or plans very often. Those few who already had a fixed idea of what sort of future profession they felt called to were exceptional and gained no following in their peer group. The master's in business administration programme at the university's newest graduate school was gaining adherents, tempted by the vast riches which Wall Street was said to be spewing forth. But I don't believe Reggie joined that crowd, and, in fact, in later life he was to be disparaging of the MBAs which then proliferated in the financial world. Who needs an MBA to do a deal? he would ask – not expecting any answer.

But I lost touch with Reggie as we departed the halls of presumed wisdom and set out to find our feet in an increasingly slippery world, lathered now by ruthless ambition, but made no cleaner by the detergent which is competition. The struggle for jobs and then for promotion, and always for quick gains, had swept away the ethos of fair play which had previously been paramount in the great houses of Wall Street and the City of London. It was dog-eat-dog, devil take the hindmost – corners were there to be cut and loopholes to be exploited. Nevertheless, I gravitated to this world from the pull of nepotism, joining a Wall Street house where my father was a partner, but neither in New York where I began, or in London where I was soon transferred to, did I run across Reggie, so I assumed he had ventured into some other field.

It was many years later when I finally ran into him at the Travellers in Paris – that very cosmopolitan club, housed in a mock Gothic mansion built at the turn of the century for a famous courtesan by a banker lover. We caught up over lunch at the club table – long enough to allow a *tête-à-tête* conversation. By now I had become 'something in the City', a phrase much used in Victorian times, when maiden aunts were reluctant to admit that a younger son in the family was besmirching the escutcheon by working with scamps and thieves in that den of trade. Reggie started off by announcing, "I do deals!"

"Who with?" I enquired with interest.

"No one," replied Reggie. "I'm a freelancer."

"Isn't that a bit dicey? I mean from a steady income point of view."

"Ah…Maybe, but then I get to keep the whole fee. I don't need to rely on getting a piece of the bonus pool."

This was how I learnt that Reggie was now what we used to call a 'five percenters'. These existed in the nineteenth century and were originally foreign loan contractors who would exploit contacts in diplomatic circles to secure mandates for foreign loan flotations, which they would then hawk around the City, picking up a five percent commission on the amount of the issue from the accepting issuing house. One such character invented a totally fictitious South American republic, forged mandate papers and persuaded a merchant bank to handle the issue. But just in time, some clerk looked at an Atlas, and so the enterprising five percenter never collected his fee. One must remember that in those good old times, bonds issued by non-European governments were issued at par and the borrower sometimes received as little as 70% – so there was plenty of room for fat fees all around. Times have changed – evolved, some might say – and Reggie would have been lucky to receive a half of one percent commission on any business he introduced.

In casual chats with other members, I learnt that Reggie was an absolute 'whizz' at backgammon, playing to the international tournament standard. It was thought that this might be his main source of steady income, as many in the club fancied themselves at the game and were happy to sit down with Reggie at the backgammon board – after a good lunch. We have few Greek ship owners amongst the membership, and they enjoy playing for high stakes. I don't think poor Reggie was the equivalent of a pool hall hustler, but I was not going to match my modest backgammon skills against his.

It soon became apparent that my interest to Reggie was my presumed list of City contacts. He believed me to be on intimate terms with every clearing or merchant bank chairman or senior partner. After that first meeting, following several score of silent years, hardly a month went by when I did not receive a call from Reggie begging an introduction to a highly placed City figure (starting with my own firm). It was always the 'deal of the century', and my friend always had an explanation as to how it had escaped the attention of an established firm. An early example was a call I received from Reggie in Sydney. He claimed to have befriended a realtor charged with selling a property comprising a hefty piece of Tasmania. All that was needed was a million or two to secure development planning consents and begin some building before reselling the property at three times the purchase price.

"But why hasn't your friend gone to an Australian bank?" I asked, innocently.

"Because they'll take the lion's share in fees. We'll both be tail-end Charlies when it comes to doling out the goodies." Reggie's priority in life was fees and how he could garner his slice.

"What makes you think banks in London won't do the same thing?"

"Because they need us. They won't have a clue on how to work the planning consent system – which is complicated here."

"Reggie, that's just why no one here will touch it, they won't rely on your real estate agent pal to do the due diligence, nor will they sit around for the time lapses involved. I'm sorry but it's a nonstarter."

I learnt later that Reggie's friend had finally gone straight to an Australian bank, cutting Reggie out of the deal. The next was equally fanciful. Reggie claimed to have befriended a member of a large family clan who wholly owned a world-famous confectionery brand. His contact told him the family was ready to sell.

"My dear Reggie," I said, with a sigh, "this is a hoary old chestnut – everybody and his uncle has been at the… (I mentioned the name), including my own firm. The family holding is spread far and wide, the capital gains taxes would be horrendous, and a big majority of the family are dead set against selling – or even going public."

"My friend says this is changing and he can convince them."

"Have you talked to any other family member?"

"No! This has got to be top secret."

"Well, it can hardly be done on one chap's say so, for goodness's sake! Can you tell me who you are talking to?"

"Well…OK, but strictly between us – I trust you of course (he mentioned our club). Its Billy…"

"I suspected so, Reggie. I'm afraid we all know Billy. He's mortgaged his stake in the company to the hilt. He's deeply in debt and he's been running around the City and the Street trying to get personal loans, against his life insurance and his wife's shares in the company – from whom he is separated, by the way."

Poor Reggie was crestfallen, but no setback deterred him. He continued calling with the 'deal of the century' and I continued parrying his introductory lunges with as much tact as I could muster. Then there was silence for several months and I learnt that Reggie had married. This was good news I thought – perhaps Reggie would now be required to get regular work. Unless, of course, he had found an heiress or a lady of means already. With Reggie's luck, in all things other than backgammon, I feared the money might turn out to be a mirage. But soon he was in London, and he invited me to dine and meet his bride who he explained was Russian. He was careful to inform me that he was converting to the Orthodox faith. I decided he was imparting this information so that I would not suspect the lady was Jewish. I rather hoped she might be, as she would instinctively hold robust financial views and rigorously test Reggie's outlandish potential deals. But be that as it may, having Russian ancestry myself, I was more than curious. Mrs Reggie turned out to be a tall blonde, drop-dead gorgeous, as the vernacular would have it – and having spotted my own antecedents, confidentially informed me she was of 'former people' stock. That rather curious designation was invented by Stalin to describe White Russian émigrés, but many members of the old noble class had been unable or unwilling to leave after the Bolshevik Revolution and were still extant in the general population. And I was more than ready to believe the lady, who was called Ekaterina – there was no hint of peasantry in her appearance or comportment. We passed a pleasant evening, but alarm bells began to ring when Reggie took me aside and said, "I've got a fabulous deal! I'll call you tomorrow."

The next day, Reggie was on the phone asking to come and see me. He had never done this before. Our contact was always by phone. Of course, I agreed. He had not been in my room for two seconds before ushering my secretary out of the room with his gaze, his voice dropping to a conspiratorial whisper as he went to the door to ensure it was properly closed.

"Chromium Diopside!" whispered my visitor.

"Reggie, I can assure you this room is not bugged, it's soundproof and you can talk in a normal tone."

"OK, OK…but this is super-duper hush hush," continued Reggie, still glancing around the room, as if looking for a hidden microphone. "Chromium Diopside is a mineral that produces a green gemstone, so pure it is often mistaken for emerald. It has a great history. The ancient Greeks considered that wearing it increased brain power. The Chinese lap them up – all sorts of magical powers. But here's the kicker, it is only found in commercial quantities in a small mountain range in deepest Siberia, not far from the Chinese border, and it can only be mined three months in the year."

"Sounds jolly," I said. "When do we start?"

"This is no joke!" replied a shocked Reggie. "Cat (I assumed he was referring to his lovely wife) has a cousin who has a friend who owns the only licence to extract Chromium Diopside in private hands – and he's willing to sell."

"Let me guess," I said. "He wants US dollars or any foreign currency for it."

"That's it."

"And there is exchange control in Russia."

"Yes...but we've got a way around that. Cat sets up a personal holding company in Cyprus. Russians can do that to hold foreign currency they have earned abroad. There is even a double tax treaty between Russia and Cyprus. Cat's company then bills the bank here in US dollars for consulting services in an amount equivalent to the consideration for the licence. Her cousin's friend sets up his own Cyprus holding company and transfers the licence to it. Cat then buys it from his company in US dollars and, hey presto, we've got the licence, and we cede 49% to the bank, and they get their money back, plus a big up tick, 'cause these gemstones sell like hot cakes."

"I take it there is a prohibition on foreign ownership of exploitation rights to Chromium Diopside."

"Yes – but Cat's Cyprus company – our company (obviously you will get a piece of the action) will still be Russian controlled."

I didn't know whether to laugh or cry.

"It's a total nonstarter, Reggie," I said – and he had been looking at me with the expression of a retriever bringing a picked up dead pheasant to his master.

"First of all," I began, "no bank is going to accept a false invoice for non-existent consulting services to a new Cyprus company and its principal which they don't know from Adam. Secondly, even if you could persuade a bank to advance the money, they would hardly accept half the asset purchased with an uncertain future revenue stream, as reasonable collateral. Thirdly, the transfer to a Cyprus company of the mining licence would be illegal – they're only supposed to hold external revenue or assets. Finally, the arrangement would not pass the test of regulations prohibiting foreign ownership of Chromium Diopside mines. In fact, your deal has so many holes in it, you could use it as a colander to drain the pasta."

Now Reggie's expression changed to that of the retriever who, having dropped the pheasant, gets no pat from his master.

I learnt later that Ekaterina had set up a Cyprus holding company, but her cousin's friend had sold his licence to a Siberian mining company for a reasonable consideration in rubles. But the Cyprus company had figured in other Russian deals that Reggie insisted on bringing to me – his tail wagging with another 'deal of the century'. One involved the adaptation of a new drug for treating wound shock trauma in animals to human use. Another involved shipping Arctic icebergs in great barges to the Black Sea and piping the melted water to Persia. There was no end to Reggie's deal-making imagination.

Then the flow stopped, and I saw or heard no more of Reggie and Ekaterina. One day I was lunching at the Travellers in Paris, when someone on the club table said: "Have you heard about Reggie?" I feared the worse. But my informant continued.

"He's finally in the chips! You know that Russian girl he married? Ekaterina something? Well, she turns out to be a sort of double agent. She has been working for the NKVD sniffing out illegal currency and other fraudulent deals involving Cyprus, the favourite domicile of Russia overseas holding companies. Well, she was also recruited by the FBI as a special agent investigating money laundering and reporting to the US Treasury. Apparently, the Russians knew all about it and were happy, on condition she shared info involving Russian money laundering folks. Well…wait for this! The US Treasury pays a bounty to anyone bringing a money laundering miscreant to heel, including to foreigners *pour encourager les autres*, and Ekaterina made this part of her deal when she signed on with the FBI. Money laundering always involves US dollars and so the Americans claim jurisdiction worldwide and sequester the ill-gotten gains anywhere. The bounty is 10% of the money recovered. This Russian lass came across a hoard of one hundred million dollars, which the Treasury was able to grab, and she walked away with ten million US dollars as her bounty. Of course, her cover is blown, and they are living in retirement on the Cap d'Antibes. Reggie comes in here from time to time."

I picked up my glass and drank a silent toast to Reggie. He had married his 'deal of the century'.

FINIS

Eleventh Tale

The Croupier

Once I loved a girl. I loved her passionately, madly, wholly – without any qualifications. I loved her with every fibre of my body and every spirit of my soul. I loved every aspect of her, whether physical or intellectual. I loved her body, her face, her voice; I loved her wit, her humour, her moods. There was nothing about her I did not love – no aspect of her character or her personality. She could do nothing, say nothing, think nothing to change or reduce my love.

The only question that touched on my love, the only dilemma that I faced in my all-consuming love, was which of the strands that made up its golden cord was paramount. Was it the physical love, in its garment of pure lust? Or a spiritual love, which gloried in her flowering mind? The physical I had encountered first. Her form was perfection but soon I was able to take in her face and, most importantly, her expression. Her forehead, cheekbones, straight nose and mouth that turned up at the corners, could have been the product of a sculptor from ancient Greece, rather than Nature itself. But I maintain that expression is the highest percentile of beauty, and hers shone through the liquid brightness of her azure eyes as a window on an inner beauty – honouring its external form. Her voice was not merely heard, it thrilled like the pipes of Pan on a summer morn. Her walk, her gestures, her very presence were stanzas of poetry in motion. But attempts to analyse my love – to understand its composition, as one might seek the recipe for a favourite dish – this fruitless preoccupation was subsumed in an even greater question which burned in me: did she love me?

I must explain myself. I am a croupier, and the full and impressive name of my employer is *La Société des Bains de Mer et le Cercle des Étrangers à Monaco*, now usually referred to simply as SBM. It owns the world-famous casino in Monte Carlo. Of course, its major shareholder is our Prince. Some of you will remember the great battle between Onassis, once the second largest shareholder in SBM, and our Prince, over the future strategy of the business. The Greek wanted the casino and its attendant activities to remain exclusive, whereas our Prince wanted it to be more open to the public at large and thus increase revenue. It is an indisputable fact that in any dispute between even the richest of men and the Sovereign – the winner will always be the Sovereign.

You may imagine that as a simple croupier in a casino, I was insignificant, and therefore my love was so as well. I will disabuse you of that impression if you allow. It is often said that the people of the Principality of Monaco are either policemen or croupiers. The only reasonable basis for this slur is that we do have the largest number of policemen per capita of any independent country. There are good reasons for this, but it is not my intention to lecture on the history and condition of my country. But I can at least explain where I stand in its society.

Our family, the Frangiotti, are of Genovese origin, as are the Grimaldi, our Royal family. But to be brutally frank, the Grimaldi were not much better than pirates who sheltered in the bay that is now Monaco, whereas the Frangiotti were knights in the service of the Republic of Genoa, and – as mercenaries, for the Dukes of Savoy – now the Royal family of Italy. Within the Ligurian tribe based in Genoa, the Grimaldi were Guelfs and the Frangiotti were Ghibbelines, and these two fought a bitter civil war, during which the Grimaldi were clever enough to gain title to Monaco, eventually recognised by the Kingdom of Sardinia.

My father, Colonel Giovanni Frangiotti was the Second Commander of the *Compagnie des Carabiniers du Prince* – the First Commander being the Prince himself. This is all we have as a standing army – only some 300 officers and men, who, together with the *Compagnie des Sapeurs Pompier* and the Police, comprise our defence force. The main duty of the *Carabiniers* is to supply the Palace Guard. Naturally, my father was a high member of the Court and an intimate friend of the Prince. My father is now retired, but I am often received at Court, because of my father and as a member of one of Monaco's principal families. You may josh at the Monegasques as merely croupiers and policemen, but under the foreign riff raff which now comprise most of our population, we do have a society of our own.

I have entered, somewhat unwillingly, into this history lest you think my love for Celine – yes, that is her name – was unworthy. Celine was the daughter of the chairman of *Compagnie Monegasque de Banque,* our most prestigious bank. He is a Frenchman called Armand Beauregard. Celine and I were social equals; however, you might disdain my occupation, but did she? Of course, my father wanted me to go into public service – the police perhaps, which he thought had more varied prospects that the Carabiniers. But I was not inspired. In a strange way, I thought I would see the world with the SBM, and I did, working in the company's casinos in the Middle East and even assisting in training croupiers from casinos around the world. My father complained of my lack of ambition. He would have liked to see me behind a desk in the management offices of SBM. But I liked being a croupier. I was rapid with numbers. I liked dealing *vingt et un* and baccarat. Spinning the wheel was rather boring but the observation of the motley crowd of player was endlessly fascinating. Of course, standards had plummeted, particularly in dress. And we now had lady croupiers, an innovation I disparaged because I felt it demeaning for the fairer sex which should be on pedestals – not sharing the lesser roles of we men.

I feel you question the relevance of all this self-analysis to my story. But I question it as well. I was always a confident young man, secure in my position, and comfortable with my occupation. When I dreamt it was of a pleasant future, of kindly fate which placed me in such salubrious surroundings, of family and friends. What changed? What put my self-esteem in jeopardy? Was it my all-consuming love for Celine? It could not be otherwise. Was I worthy of her? That was the question which tormented me and poisoned my life. I can explain how we met. No, that is inconsequential – of course we met as children, Monegasque society is miniscule. What is important is how we continued to meet or didn't meet, when such was my overwhelming and sole desire. There are frequent occasions at the Palace when our local worthies are invited and received by the Prince. Celine and I were always amongst these, I was fully acquainted with the Prince. If my father was absent, frequently as he aged, the Prince never failed to ask me of news of him. He could see that Celine and I were usually together. We were of the same generation. I imagine he thought we were sweethearts. Naturally, he took much more notice of Celine because she was a young and beautiful girl and the Prince, still unmarried then, was well known for his proclivities in that direction. Then, Celine and I met at other formal occasions where the local population were expected to turn out, at tennis tournaments, in the stands at the finish of the Grand Prix. I saw her alone as well, sometimes frequently. She lunched with me – even dining on my few evenings off. I took her sailing on her father's neat sloop, and we met at the beach. We played tennis together, we walked together, and I taught her to play golf. We did all things one does in the playground that is Monaco. She knew full well I loved her but didn't appreciate with what intensity. She took it for granted but not in a proud way. Her kindness allowed for no such pride, but she could not help but think it was natural that I should love her. What favours did she grant me? The occasional kiss, returned with friendly interest – but not with passion. I was afraid to press her. I feared resistance. Should my passion exceed hers – should I suddenly feel a cooling of whatever warmth greeted my physical advances, I would retire in panic – my ardour melted away.

Of the panoply of emotions associated with my love, jealousy had not been one. You notice I speak of the past. I basked in the admiration which Celine attracted in any surrounding. The Prince was only the most distinguished of the many which accorded Celine the glances and stares of such admiration. I felt pride, not jealousy. I remember still when this underwent a tragic transformation. I remember it because there is not a moment when it did not return to my mind in an image of agonising intensity. I was like the drowning man whose life flashes before him, except that it was that moment that flashed and overrode any other thought I might have. It was that incident, amongst all that followed, that, without extinguishing the fire that was my love, created an accompanying glacier of hate.

We were attending a Royal reception for the world-famous tennis stars competing in the Open Championship. The Prince was hosting, of course. He even joked with me. "You would defeat these on your tables, my dear Frangiotti, but they are winners in their profession."

I replied, "I have never seen them risk their winnings with me, my Prince." This shows you what terms I was on with my sovereign. I could see Celine very engaged in conversation with one of the players. I will not name him. I cannot name him. I was on duty that day at the Casino but had negotiated a leave of absence for a few hours to attend this reception. The *Chef des Croupiers* was always lenient with me. As the son of my father, I was always a rather favoured employee at SMB. I thought it natural that Celine should assist in entertaining these tennis players. Celine had lost her mother early in life, and she acted as hostess in her father's house, and felt herself to be a representative of his bank at social occasions.

But then, out of the corner of my eye, as I was speaking to another guest, I saw Celine and the tennis player turn to leave the room. The reception was in the grand ballroom of the Casino, and I immediately thought Celine might be taking the guest to investigate the main room of play (*salle des jeux*) and so I followed, thinking I might act as a guide. But soon I realised, still some steps behind them, that they were turning toward the exit. They then held hands as they went down the stairs that lead to the *Place du Casino*. I followed, my mouth dry and my heart beating. There are taxis there, but Celine and the tennis star turned left and walked the short way to the *Hôtel de Paris*. I followed, staying well back. At the door they were greeted by Edouard, the doorman, who I knew well. He assisted the revolving door from which they passed inside. I stood in a corner waiting for Edouard to be occupied with an arriving taxi. I then slipped into the hall. The concierge spotted me and gave me a curt nod, and quickly looked away, this surprised me. I expected to be greeted – we were friends. But clearly, he was not pleased to see me. I scanned the hall for the couple, I looked furtively in the bar, in the empty restaurant. Celine and the tennis player were nowhere to be found. The full realisation of what had happened struck me like lightning. I could hardly breathe. I fled! I ran from the hotel, almost knocking down Edouard, and crossed the Place, still running, with cars sounding their horns at me. A phrase began to repeat in my head, like the chorus in an oratorio. "The tennis player has possessed Celine – and I have not!" I sat at the sidewalk café, which is opposite the *hôtel*, where I knew Celine to be with a lover. I ordered a cognac and tried to stop the phrase repeating and scarring my brain.

After a second cognac, listening to those words in my head, I rose and slowly dragged myself around the Place to the other side. It felt as if I was not walking properly, and people stopped and stared. One asked me if I was ill. I stood in front of the famous pawn shop, where on the window is still a legend written in the Russian Cyrillic. From there I could see people coming and going from the entrance of the Hôtel de Paris. Soon I saw Celine leave. She walked with that light step I knew so well. She was carrying the straw bonnet she had been wearing at the reception. Edouard the doorman waved to a taxi. Celine got in and they drove off.

From that dreadful day, my life changed. I was not Luca Frangiotti anymore. I was a strange creature with terrible thoughts, and that phrase overcrowded my brain to bursting. I was a zombie. I went through my work as an automaton. The strangest thing of all was that I still saw Celine. We did the same things we had always done. Of course, she saw and felt my altered mood, but it could not have been as evident to her as it was to me. Her enquiries were brief, mundane: "Are you unwell? You seem tired. Shall we rest?" And my monosyllabic replies seemed to satisfy her. It goes without saying that neither of us made any allusion to that fateful reception for the famous tennis players. When I looked now at her extraordinarily beautiful face, I longed to scream, "That tennis player has possessed you and I have not!" The phrase that haunted me.

But there was worst to come, although the mysterious aspect of it was that it did not seem worse. Her first crime in my eyes overshadowed the others. I had taken to following her, like a pathetic stalker, the hatred of myself still dominating a new hatred that was growing like a cancer. I reasoned with myself in an obtuse and stupid way that I was now always with Celine. When we were not together, I was discreetly behind her. I knew my town so well that I could follow her unobserved. One day, I followed her to the very gates of the princely palace. I expected her to be stopped by the *Carabinier* on guard. He merely saluted and she passed through. I waited three hours – yes, three hours – but I was strangely unmoved by the significance of what I was observing. Mentally, I was shrugging my shoulders. I still thought mainly of the tennis player and the *Hôtel de Paris*, and only as a sort of side thought, I said to myself, "She is the mistress of the Prince." It was as though I was making a casual observation to that other self – that person that was Luca Frangiotti – before the tennis player. I observed further visits and they seemed to decline in importance. My senses were numb by now. It was the same feeling as a limb that goes numb – the circulation cut off from its position while asleep. My consciousness suffered in just the same way.

Then occurred an event which stunned and delighted my countrymen. The Prince went to America, fell in love with a famous film actress and married her. She was of Irish peasant stock and very beautiful. Our royal family is too minor to insist on royal alliances in marriage. The wedding took place in our Cathedral in front of guests from European royal families and celebrities from America. But there was a luncheon after where the Monegasque notables were invited, including our parents with Celine and me. There were round tables and we sat with M. Beauregard, my parents, and the current Commander of the *Caribiniers*. The Prince had been married in the uniform of First Commander of the *Compagnie*. But I sat like a dumb throughout. No one at the table noticed, but a hair trigger had been pulled, and my soul had exploded into the horrible realisation that I must kill Celine. Yes! Kill Celine! I sense the shock that now comes over those who will read this like a tsunami from an oceanic earthquake. But I ask you – I implore you to await my explanation! I still loved Celine. Yes, I loved her as I had always done, I invite you to re-read the opening paragraphs of this manuscript, where I described how I loved Celine. Every word of it remains true. I retract nothing. The new hatred that had been gnawing at my entrails for weeks was not a hatred of Celine; it was a hatred of what Celine had done – a hatred of the tennis player, of the *Hôtel de Paris*, of Edouard the doorman, of the concierge, of the *Caribinier* at the Palace gate – of my Prince! But wait still! I must explain about the trigger that detonated the horrible charge within me. You must understand how I had been brought to this.

Before we sat down to luncheon, the newly married Royal couple had received us in the full flush of the occasion's excitement. In the receiving line, Celine went before me, and I watched her make a deep curtsy to our new Princess. Then, as I bent over the hand of the Princess, I could still see, in the corner of my eye, Celine repeating her courtly greeting to the Prince. As I straightened up, so did Celine rising from her curtsy, the Prince still holding her hand. But then I spied in a flash, in the wink of an eye, the briefest of glances between them. But it was not a glance, even if hardly lasting a tenth of a second. It was a look exchanged between them. It was not the look a sovereign might exchange with a loyal subject. No! It was the look of a man telling his mistress: "Do not worry, nothing has changed." And I knew instantly when I saw it that the Prince intended that Celine remain his mistress and that she was acquiescing.

So now you know why I sat like a dumb at the luncheon that followed. I began to plan the denouement of this nightmare. When the wedding celebrations would have ended, and the captains and the kings departed, I would ask Celine to spend the day with me. We would play tennis, have a light lunch at the tennis club and then go for a sail. At lunch, no doubt, Celine would chat about the wedding, the Princess's wedding gown, the guests and so on. Then we would set sail towards our watery grave. The gentle waves of the blue Mediterranean would lap against the sides of the boat, and a whispering wind would ruffle our main sail. And then, looking lovingly into Celine's azure eyes. I would dispatch her and, immediately myself. Together, forever together, we would sink to that other place, and surrounded by the fires of Hell, I would finally possess Celine…

Note from the Translator

The manuscript above was written in a rather stilted French, suggesting, I imagine, a Jesuit education. I have attempted to reproduce in my translation the personality and behaviour of the author. But I have found it a very difficult task and must admit that the original language achieves a more accurate depiction of the unusual thoughts and actions recounted.

For good orders' sake, I must relate the circumstances that completed the tragedy. The sailboat belonging to M. Beauregard was found drifting crew-less by a patrol boat of the Carabinieri. A day later, two bodies washed ashore at Monte-Carlo beach. They were identified as Mlle Celine Beauregard, daughter of the boat's owner – the chairman of Compagnie Monegasque de Banque, and M. Luca Frangiotti, an employee of the Société de Bains de Mer, and member of a prominent Monegasque family. In the boat had been found this manuscript and a tennis racquet – the edges of which were bloody. The autopsy's revealed that Mlle Beauregard had first been bludgeoned to death, or perhaps merely to unconsciousness, by the racquet, before being thrown overboard. The type of the blood on the racquet matched that of the victim. M. Frangiotti had either fallen, or thrown himself, overboard immediately after. The deaths appeared to be virtually simultaneous.

FINIS

Twelfth Tale

The Honest Pursuit

Major Sir George St Ansell Mortimer Fortescue Brake, 10th Baronet began on the second boiled egg of his leisurely breakfast. He rather preferred his eggs poached, but he enjoyed the use of a silver gadget which crops the end of the egg, a very ancient wedding present. As he was performing this pleasurable operation, Mrs Breakspear entered with a fresh piece of toast, already cut into 'soldiers'.

"Coffee still nice and hot, Sir George?" she enquired, feeling the Meissen coffee pot.

"All in good order as usual, Mrs Breakspear," replied the baronet, as he refolded the Times for ease of plate-side reading.

This good lady was the daughter of a former gamekeeper on the Brake estate, and now the wife of the local publican. She 'did' for Sir George in his village cottage, making his breakfast every day and cleaning twice a week. The baronet's current, modest residence was a consequence of the death and taxes which had forced the sale of the Brake estate, encompassing the small village of Brakeford. The 8th Baronet had been killed at the age of 35 at the siege of Lady-smith in the Anglo-Boer War, and then the 9th on the Western Front in the First Great War. The present holder of the title had been too young for the Second War but had survived Korea and distinguished himself with the Gloucester's at the Imjin River. But by the late '60s, 'the game was up', as Sir George liked to put it. Coutts, now owned by a clearing bank, would no longer carry the huge overdraft ballooned by inheritance taxes. Brake Hall and its 7,000 acres did not come close to washing its face. The Hall, its walls increasingly denuded of the old masters sold in a vain attempt to carry on, was not of sufficient importance to be open to the public. The cost of staff, indoors and out, had become prohibitive. Almost in tears, the gallant Major had arranged the move of the Brake Hounds to new Kennels a few miles away and resigned his mastership.

The estate was quite quickly sold to an American investment banker, originally on the strength of its outstanding shooting, but eventually as a residence, when the banker, together with legions of compatriots, moved to the city to join in its Americanisation. The new squire, Harry Macleod by name, was very keen to befriend Sir George and offered him a paid consulting role for the management of the estate which Sir George tactfully declined with thanks, assuring that he would always be at his disposal for free advice. Mr MacLeod was, like all good Americans, much divorced, and his most recent ex was enjoying her generous alimony in Palm Beach and Southampton. He had one daughter at school, but no current wife to demand immediate alterations. So, he relied on the baronet mostly for help with the gamekeeper and game management. Harry was essentially a shooting man, but the baronet was greatly relieved to find his neighbour was understanding about foxes, and, in any case, had no intention of commercialising the shoot.

Sir George had managed to extract a handful of cottages in the village from the sale of the estate. Harry MacLeod had indicated that he had no use for them. At one point, the family had owned the entire village. Sir George had moved into the nicest of the cottages and the rent from the remaining properties supplemented his army pension. He was widowed soon after his return from Korea. His wife Jane, a distant cousin, had borne him one son, and her loss, together with the forced sale of the estate, had weighed heavily on him for some time. He had one sister, Gwendolyn, married to an equally impecunious squire down in deepest Cornwall, and several cousins spread throughout what was once the British Empire. In fact, if Sir George's only son William were to die before begetting a son, the heir to the baronetcy would have to consider giving up his sheep farming in New Zealand. With an estate in England to come home to, one assumes the consideration would be brief.

But it is with young William, or Billy as he was universally known, that we are concerned here. Motherless at an early age, affected by the loss of his first home, Billy had not settled easily. Physically well setup, with a masculine version of his mother's beauty, he was not *omnes omnia bona dicere* – not all spoke well of him. He had difficulty making and keeping friends. Very attractive to women, he was soon critical of any who sought his affection. Any interest in a subject or activity faded quickly. An unusual and overriding aspect of his character was an obsession with fairness. All children have an instinctive feeling for equity. The expression 'It isn't fair!' is well-known to mothers and nannies but most grow up to realise that justice is heavily mitigated by circumstances and the realities of life in general. But Billy carried the grudge of unfairness into school and his later attempts to settle into a career path. At Harrow, he castigated the masters disrespectfully for what he perceived to be discipline applied unfairly. This, together with a lack of concentration and surly behaviour, risked expulsion at one point.

Up at King's College, Cambridge, Billy had matured and gained a bit of a following as he had a natural charm. But his social and romantic life suffered from a suspicious side that was always on the lookout for some examples of injustice. If a girl he asked out made the traditional excuse of having to wash her hair, he suspected she was planning to go out with another beau. The little white lies that are a necessity to smooth social intercourse became monstrous lies to Billy Brake. He soon began to identify the myriad little dishonesties that lurk amid academic life. Billy's tutor was subjected to minute examination for signs of hypocrisy – any prevarication on his part raised suspicions in the mind of his pupil.

Whilst up, Billy had given little thought to a career. The Army seemed obvious, but he could not put any more financial pressure on his father, who had struggled to pay for his education. And the Army was changing, Sir George noted with chagrin; captains and majors were retiring early, promotion was more difficult and outside jobs evaporated beyond the age of 30. The British officer corps was drawn from the moneyed class – a class greatly reduced in number, particularly by the First Great War, and now far less moneyed after the Second. No, the Army wouldn't do, and his father agreed with regret.

But at Cambridge, Billy had found an extra-curricular interest. He had excelled in amateur dramatics. His looks, voice and presence marked him out as a born actor and, coming down with a minimal degree, he was encouraged to apply for RADA, and to his father's astonishment, was accepted. Although Billy did well, it took the efforts of elder mentors to persuade him that he could not achieve star billing in the West End before first serving an apprenticeship in repertory. Unfortunately, with increased confidence had come impatience, a trait which was to become more apparent. Early success in any endeavour raised unreasonable expectations in Billy, who inevitably suspected systematic unfairness was holding him back. This poisoned both his relationships with colleagues and his further development as an actor, and his agent who tried to counsel him suffered the same fate as his Tutor at Cambridge. On a visit home to his father, he announced he was 'chucking it' even though he had done rather well in a minor role at the Bristol Old Vic.

What to do next became the dominant preoccupation. On a few home visits, Billy had befriended Holly MacLeod, the daughter of the new neighbour at Brake Hall. She was more than a comely lass. In fact, as Virgil puts it: *vera incestu potuit Dea* (the true goddess was evident in her step) or – to put it in her own American vernacular – she was drop dead gorgeous. She was also very horsey, having been educated at Foxcroft, a chic private school in Virginia that allowed the pupils to keep horses. Holly had spent time at a Swiss finishing school, a junior year abroad in Paris from her American college and was learned and sophisticated. Sir George had become quite close to his successor at the Hall, who valued his friendship and advice, but he had some unexpressed concerns about the possibility of a romantic attachment between Billy and Holly. In addition to a good deal of hacking around estate, one-or two-days hunting with the Brake, mounted always from Holly's impressive string, she had also taken him racing. Billy found himself with two options for further employment, both pressed on him with enthusiasm. Holly wanted him to be apprenticed to their trainer – Mr MacLeod had a few National Hunt horses in training, whereas he urged him to go into the City. On discussing these ideas with his father, Billy quickly observed that Mr MacLeod had not offered him a job with his own firm – a fact that immediately aroused his suspicions, and so he opted for the training yard.

It did not take Billy long to notice that racing was not as pure as the driven snow. An isolated case of a 'bent jockey' made an impression – even though it was on the flat and had nothing to do with his own yard. Although Billy worked hard to learn, his heart was not really in it, particularly when he realised that it would be some years, if ever, before he could set up as a trainer on his own with a full book of generous owners. Clearly, he must now try the City. And so, back in Brakebury for a stay, he poured his heart out to Holly who asked her father to give Billy some introductions in the City. The charming Holly was an American girl like almost all-American girls, combining, quite unconsciously, the roles of mother, big sister, psychoanalyst, mentor, father confessor, spiritual guide, social organiser, occasional lover, and potential wife. At this stage, Holly was still holding the last two roles in reserve, which was quite natural, as American girls feel that all the previous roles must be fully exercised before choosing a mate for either casual and temporary purposes, or as a future supplier of alimony payments. Billy Brake was entirely comfortable with this stage of their relationship and had to admit to himself that he had yet to find anything duplicitous about Holly MacLeod.

Her father, Harry MacLeod, set Billy up with a jobber on the London Stock Exchange and he set to learning all he could about the trading of stocks and shares. His new boss, Joe Lowy, a very respected figure on the Floor, did not immediately amuse him with a hoary old Stock Exchange joke that he liked to tell newcomers. It seems a broker approached a jobber in Cons Gold shares to ask a dealing price. The broker was wearing a straight black tie, a black armband and had a document looking very much like a probate form sticking out of his pocket. The jobber read him as a seller settling the estate of a deceased and quoted him accordingly.

"I'll take a thousand," said the broker.

"What?" exclaimed the jobber. "I thought you were settling an estate."

The broker replied, "I am but my client died a bear."

For the uninitiated, 'bears' are pessimistic sellers, and 'bulls' are optimistic buyers. The broker's client had sold Cons Gold shares short, expecting a fall in price and his executor was now covering the position. By appearing as a seller when he was a buyer, the broker had 'picked up' the jobber. The interplay between brokers and jobbers is part of a process that maintains liquidity on the stock exchange, but poor Billy immediately took this as a sign that dishonest practices were rife in his new profession. He carried on, of course, with his new working life and made a few friends – through Joe Lowy, a jovial Jewish gentleman very well versed in Stock Exchange lore. Billy liked the club-like nature of the City and its traditions. He sampled a good deal of London night life without straying towards excess and was soon elected to his father's West End club. But again, he could not help ruminating on the obvious fact that he could not expect to enter partnership with Joe Lowy – or any other firm, without a contribution of capital, and it would take years to achieve a partnership on merit alone.

And so, it was back to the consoling counselling of Holly MacLeod. By now his relationship with the beauteous Holly had advanced to the penultimate stage, and the advisory session took place in bed, as a healthier alternative to the traditional post coital cigarette. Holly was propped up on one elbow, stroking, and sometimes gently thumping his chest – to emphasise certain points.

"The trouble with you, my dear Billy (Holly had adopted English forms of speech), is that you lack motivation." She thumped his chest. "And your obsessive search for justice in this unjust world is just a cover for your lack of motivation. And why are you unmotivated?" Holly gave him another thump on the chest. "Because you just don't really like what you're doing!" She answered her own question. "And…because you're unmotivated – don't like what you're doing – you're impatient. Why are you impatient?" Holly used the so called 'Q&A' format in her counselling sessions. "Because you want to get it over quickly – you don't really like the gallop, so you want to get to the finish line as soon as possible."

Billie lay there on his back, staring at the frescoed ceiling in one of Brake Hall's best bedrooms, wishing this session could be over so that he could prove his motivation with another amorous bout.

Having read his mind, Holly continued:

"And allow me to say, my darling, sweetest, ever-loving Billy, you make love too fast. Don't you like it?"

"Good grief! These American girls!" Billy said to himself – and he turned his attention away from the frescoed ceiling and proceeded to show he had learnt teacher's lesson.

But later over tea, in the drawing room lavishly refurbished by a smart West End decorator, Holly had another suggestion.

"Why don't you ask your Auntie Gwen for some country job in Cornwall? I don't want to lose you from here, but I don't think your old man wants you hanging about."

By now, Billy had grown accustomed to her face but also to Holly's ways, so he did as he was told. Aunt Gwendolyn was delighted. Childless herself, she doted on her nephew and had followed the fits and starts of his career with dismay.

"Estate Agency!" She barked at her brother in a subsequent telephone conversation. "He's good-looking, well-spoken, well-dressed – just right to gain the confidence of buyers and sellers. And he's been on the Stock Exchange! Selling shares and houses is much of a muchness, isn't it?"

"I'm not so sure about that," said Sir George, "but I suppose he could do his estate agency thing here."

"No, he could not, George! Good gracious, a Brake flogging property in the Brake country? Not the done thing at all."

Sir George never argued with his sister on matters of protocol, social correctness and all that sort of thing. And so, Billy was dispatched to Cornwall and placed with the local estate agent, who would do anything to accommodate Lady Tregowan, the esteemed wife of Sir Francis Tregowan, Bt. But one must wonder at the naiveté of all concerned with this project. If there is one economic activity unsuitable to anyone with an obsessive and overly meticulous concern for absolute, undiluted honesty and fairness in all representations – it is estate agency. It took a very few visits to properties on the books, and a simple comparison with the details printed in the relevant circulars, to convince Billy that poetic licence was driven to extremes in the business of selling houses. It was also explained to him that it was not only permissible but recommended practice to show a house with six bedrooms to someone looking for a house with only three.

"But aren't we wasting every one's time?" asked Billy.

"Not a bit!" assured his boss Captain Tregear, who was retired from the Catering Corps and wore a pencil moustache. "You never know what they'll bite at. Don't forget – clients don't know their own mind. If you go for it, you can sell them a spoon when they want a fork."

Well, after a couple of months of 'going for it', Billy decided that estate agents were as bent as a tearoom spoon. Aunt Gwendolyn was very sad, as she had much enjoyed having her nephew to stay – and he made a fourth at bridge with her sister-in-law, a widow in straightened circumstances – as they used to say, who was now living permanently in the Tregowan manor house. But a further aspect of his new occupation was displeasing to Billy. He often found himself handling the sale of a property, which had been in the same family for generations, to some new City tycoon or – worse still – to a foreigner who would make little attempt to fit in locally. *Pace* his now beloved Holly, it had an uncomfortable familiar ring. And so, the world, and in particular Cornwall, lost a promising estate agent.

Back at the cottage in Brakebury, everyone was concerned with the future of Billy, including, prominently, Holly MacLeod, who agreed that a long moment of reflection on home ground would be beneficial to the eventual 11th Baronet. Looking back, a critical moment in the future evolution of our hero, was a visit to the Brake kennels he made with his father. Sir George maintained, with the total approbation of the current master, a high degree of responsibility for the breeding of the Brake hounds. The Brake was a spin-off in the early nineteenth century from the Berkeley – like several West Country packs. Sir George and his ancestors had been particularly attentive to the quality of hounds and were frequent winners at the main Hound Shows. A good many prize hounds in neighbouring packs had lines back to Brake General '51. It was true, Sir George complained, that his breeding counsel was handicapped by the fact that he no longer saw hounds hunting. He relied very heavily on the professional huntsman Sydney Biggles in this respect. It is only as one observes hounds dealing with different scenting conditions and terrain, that informed breeding decisions can be made. Sir George was a popular judge at Puppy Shows which kept him in touch with current trends, but he liked to say that looking at hounds 'on the flags', or as a car follower, is no match for hunting them, or watching them being hunted on the field.

But Sydney Biggles had no sooner greeted this young Brake on this momentous visit before he started on the subject, bringing certain hounds out on to the flags, biscuits in his kennel coat pocket, moving them about, exchanging comments with Sir George, and with a tact and respect natural to hunt servants, including Billie in the chatter – as if he must be an inheritor of hound knowledge, his line going back to the earliest baronet to carry a horn. Young Billy Brake, 11th to be, was entranced. He was more than entranced – he was converted.

A comment dropped somewhere in the conversation by Sir George to his son, to make sure of his attention, was like the seminal point in a sermon that makes the sinner throw off his evil ways. "You see," said his father, to nods from Sydney Biggles, "a hound never knowingly lies." This phrase resonated in Billy's mind like an Alpine echo. "A hound never knowingly lies!" What is meant by this is that when a hound 'gives tongue' meaning speaks (or barks – as you might say), it is because it has picked up the scent. Not that hounds don't make mistakes; the classic one being hunting 'heel'. This is the trace of scent left by the fox and pursued in the direction from which he came, rather than in the direction in which he is going. And hounds are known to 'riot', distracted by a competing scent of hares or deer. Foxes very frequently outsmart the hounds and their huntsman, but the process of hunting quarry with hounds, steeped in ancient history, can best be describes as genuine. To how many human activities can we allocate that compliment?

That evening, Holly came to dinner at the Cottage, her father being occupied, as usual, with some City function. The three discussed one single subject, until one o'clock in the morning, when Billy escorted Holly back to the Hall – staying, I fear, for a length of time Mrs Breakspear would have considered improper – before returning almost as a summer dawn was breaking. And during this mind-bending dinner, Billy heard his father, with Holly in rapt attention, discourse on hunting; reminiscing, dropping pearls of wisdom, complaining of lowered standards, explaining finer points of horses and hounds, touching on the casting of hounds, recounting famous runs, describing climactic conditions, suitable or not – a panoply of knowledge and experience.

He often addressed Holly, as though acknowledging a degree of awareness in his son as a compliment.

"You know, my dear Holly, everybody always wants to know about scent. Why are there good days and bad days? Sometimes there seems to be no connection with weather or temperature. And why in that covert or field and not that one? It's a lovely mystery and there are a thousand theories." Sir George puffed on his cigar, looked at it, and then continued.

"There's a nice story about an American MFH, Thomas Hitchcock, Senior, father of Tommy, Junior, the ten-goal polo player – which you should like, Holly. One day he was in a train trying to explain scent to someone and he put on a damp over coat and blew a big puff of cigar smoke. Then he took off the overcoat and blew another puff over his dry jacket. Then he observed the different action of the smoke. 'The coat's the ground and the cigar smoke is the scent, do you see?' Then he opened the train window and blew another puff. "That's what wind does to scent."

"How lovely, Sir George," said Holly, "I had some days with the Blue Ridge at home – and I'm going to start seriously here next season."

"That's a Virginia pack, I believe," said Sir George. "You Yanks are big on hunting – you drafted English hounds – George Washington was one of the first. Now we're bringing American crossbreeds back here to cross as we did with Welsh hounds as a while ago. So, it's not just hands across the sea, it's hounds across the sea, as well." Sir George gave a hearty laugh.

It was obvious to the ever-observant Holly that Sir George was taking a far greater interest in his son's new interest than he had in the abortive career options of the recent past. Like a sculptress looking at a mound of moist clay, Holly could visualise the statue she was about to carve. With Billy in his new frame of mind, she had something to work on. And she lost no time. Billy spent the rest of the summer in the absorption of as much hunting knowledge as his waking hours could absorb. With Holly in close attendance, he haunted book shops and libraries for books on hunting. They spent hours at the kennels. Sydney Biggles had never known ladies to take such interest in hounds – they mostly hunted to ride, rather than riding to hunt. The current master and his lady wife had more invitations to dine at Brake Hall than they could cope with – and their fellow guests seemed to be always neighbouring masters and other hunting enthusiasts. It became known that anyone keen and knowledgeable about hunting could be sure of a nice pub lunch at the Brake Arms with Holly and Billy. They went far and wide examining and buying horses for Billy – and Sir George became alarmed and embarrassed to discover that it was usually Holly's cheque book that was produced when a sale was agreed. But the sight of the two schooling their acquisitions over painted poles in the ring, their contagious enthusiasm, their immersion in what was, after all, his own favourite pastime, quelled any concerns.

Harry MacLeod took time off from his City pre-occupations to express mild concern at his daughter's new 'hobby', as he termed it and Billy was unsure whether he was the hobby, or hunting. Of course, it was both. But the new Squire was more than bemused when he found himself cornered by the two young people one evening after dinner at the Hall.

"Daddy! Listen," Holly began, "when cub hunting starts, you must let hounds into our converts."

"But Tony Stopem (the gamekeeper) says that will disturb the young pheasants," remonstrated Mr MacLeod.

"That's the whole point, Daddy, it will give them a good fly."

"You see, sir," interjected Billy, "it's like a mother hawk pushing her chicks out of the nest to make them fly."

"Yes, but Tony says they'll just fly next door and deplete our stock."

"But they're not feeding next door, sir, they'll be back and fitter for your first shooting day," said Billy.

"They'll be flying better and higher," insisted Holly. "You'll see!"

"And hounds will have cut the odd cub, so there'll be less depredation and fewer for Tony to stop up before shooting," added Billy.

Tony Stopem had already noted his young mistress' new 'hobby' and was not at all surprised by his new instructions, nor was he particularly worried about pheasant loss, as his budget allowed him to outfeed the neighbouring shoots, who regularly complained he was drawing their birds.

When cub hunting started, the two love birds, having risen at dawn and, mindless of Tony's feathered stock, were happily standing at covert side, tapping their boots with their hunting whips in the traditional fashion, whilst mature hounds and cubs crashed around the woods. By now, Billy was, in his estimation at least, a full-fledged hunting man. But, as is so often the case, it took a first, memorable run to seal the bargain he now made with his future.

It was in early December, on a bright and lightly frosty day, when hounds had met in the yard behind the Brake Arms. The morning had been disappointing, with just the odd, short scramble and a brace gone to ground in a drain, leaving the terrier men with a time-consuming dig. Sydney Biggles had then proposed to the master quite a long hack to a large spinney known as the Bratch, known as an almost certain find. Sure enough, after a wait of five minutes at covert side, Billy and Holly heard that first squeal which precedes hounds opening properly, and after another minute of the woods thundering with the cry of the full pack, Sydney was blowing "gone away" and the field master was shouting "hold hard!" to a field straining on horses, some already cantering on the spot.

After what seemed an age, they were off, but only after the field master had cried, "Go on! I've got no second horse today," and so they had gone on, with Billy and Holly in front. The Bratch was on something of a rise in the ground and for few moments they could see the fox crossing a field of stubble, but quite soon he turned left-handed and out of sight, and they could only see the hounds in full cry with Sydney close behind. They were flying over stone walls in very open country, but soon entered the extensive park of an estate which marched with the Brake acres. There hounds checked in a thick wood and feathered on a ride, while Billy looked behind him to see a very diminished field, with the master, but no whipper in, who had been left behind collecting some strays. Then hounds opened again quickly, and they were off, heading for a deep valley with some made up fences, a stream winding along the bottom and small spinneys looking down from the high ground. The crossed the stream with great leaps in two places and headed up the hill at one end. The fox had crossed a road and they were now approaching an area surrounding a disused airfield from the last war. There was another brief check and then a series of gated paddocks and they could see they were riding almost parallel with the screaming pack. At one point Sydney stopped at a gate, standing in his irons to better view his hounds, and

Holly was on her feet to open it. Billy looked around and could see no one else. It was now just the three of them. What had happened to the field? But there was no time to consider this mystery. They crossed a small road again, and Billy guessed they were heading for the village of Southleach, which he knew to be seven miles from Brakebury by road. But the pace never slowed. They were back with stone fences, and though they were on plough some of the time, Billy's thoroughbred gelding and Hollie's warmblood mare took it as though they were galloping on a fine sandy beach. As they ran on the hunted fox was suddenly in view again, and it was now clear his destination was the village of Southleach. There would be another road to cross but there was a football match in progress on the village pitch immediately on the other side and Billy thought that this is going to be interesting. But with only one field to go before the road, hounds finally caught up with Reynard, who, as they say in murder mysteries, "didn't feel a thing" – a merciful and appropriate end to a great run. As they waited on almost blown and sweating horses, Holly held Sydney's as he jumped off to play that mournful call on his horn, and the hounds broke up their quarry. Only after a good five minutes did the remnants of the field, with the whipper in and a couple of hounds, make their appearance. These included the master, but not the field master who had retired after the find. The master, red faced from exertion, was quickly on his feet, as any master must be at the kill – even as a late arrival. Sydney handed the brush to the master, with a nod towards Holly, and the master duly presented it to her.

Any memorable run is described by the participants in a simple way: the distance travelled from find to kill, and the time elapsed. For those interested in the naked truth you need only deduct about 20% from these two numbers. But this run was the decider for Billy. He had finally discovered his mission in life, an occupation he could love, and a motivation pure and sustainable. The rest was highly predictable. When the season ended, Billy and Holly went to Exmoor for some culminating days with the great Captain Wallace and the Exmoor Hunt, which carries on for a week or two in the early spring. There one evening over the port, Holly informed Billy of the date of their wedding. He couldn't exactly recall having proposed – but such formalities are considered redundant by American maidens. After the nuptial festivities, organised by Holly in a manner only rivalled by a Royal wedding, Harry MacLeod tried to persuade Sir George to move to the Hall, where the couple would reside, pointing out that there was enough room for any number of fathers in law that his daughter might collect.

But the Baronet explained he was now attached to his cottage. Mrs Breakspear also refused an invitation to join the staff at the Hall at considerably enhanced compensation. Tony Stopem mastered the art of producing both high pheasants and plentiful foxes. The master of the Brake, who had succeeded Sir George on the sale of the estate, a dozen or more years ago, finally retired. And now, if you turn to the entry on the Brake Hunt in Bailey's Directory, you will see "Master: William Brake, Esq." And all because "a hound never knowingly lies."

FINIS